Thicker Than Water

Responses to Richard Rossiter's *Arrhythmia*

'It's hard not to be swept up in the intoxicating mystery of this beguiling collection of short stories from Richard Rossiter... Rossiter draws us into a compelling narrative which explores the emotional mind. Highly recommended for readers of short stories and lovers of good literature.' Candice Cappe, *Bookseller and Publisher*, 2009.

'Rossiter's collection is so rich with connections and suggested associations that reading it invites a sort of double cognisance... Collectively [the stories] work as a masterful structural feat – and a worthy example of the whole being more than the sum of its parts.' Nicola Redhouse, *Indigo*, 5, 2010.

'...a quietly impressive collection of linked stories...Rossiter writes as some professionals play tennis, 'within himself', and the modesty and restraint of the book's style is an effective foil for the drama of its contents.' Kerryn Goldsworthy, *Sydney Morning Herald*, 2010.

'Rossiter's is a contemplative and distinctive voice. His sharp observation of the lives the stories tell is often surprising, and the collection invites many re-readings.' William Yeoman, *West Australian*, 2010.

'Rossiter is a consummate stylist...his language is sparse and finely honed...the collection acquires a haunting quality, for, as with the characters themselves, beneath the surface beats the arrhythmic pulse.' *Island*, Winter, 2010.

'Rossiter's sparse and tense prose possesses a distinctively, dry, desert-like beauty.' Patrick Allington, *Australian Book Review*, April, 2010.

Thicker Than Water

a novella

RICHARD ROSSITER

UWA PUBLISHING

First published in 2014 by
UWA Publishing
Crawley, Western Australia 6009
www.uwap.uwa.edu.au

UWAP is an imprint of UWA Publishing
a division of The University of Western Australia

THE UNIVERSITY OF
WESTERN AUSTRALIA

National Library of Australia
Cataloguing-in-Publication data:

Author: Rossiter, Richard, author.

Title: Thicker than water : a novella / Richard Rossiter.

ISBN: 9781742586052 (paperback)

Dewey Number: A823.4

Cover design by Xou Creative
Typeset by J & M Typesetting
Printed by Lightning Source

This project has been assisted by the Australian Government
through the Australia Council, its arts funding and advisory body.

Australian Government

In memory of Donald Grant, 1945–2013.

Of all the privileges of love, this seemed to him to be the most affecting: to witness, in another, memories so deep they remain ineffable, glimpsed only by an intuition, by an illogical preference or an innocent desire, by a sorrow that arises out of seeming nothingness, an inexplicable longing.

Anne Michaels, *The Winter Vault*.

She knew, precisely, the path Edy took to get to her flat from the library.

Sometimes, when she was expecting him, she imagined him walking along with that easy loping stride down Bayham Street, then right at Granary Lane, left into Montague, down the pathway behind the shops into Arlington Place, then one hundred metres to the entrance to her flat on Greenland. He would press the bell down below and she would let him in. She could hear his footsteps coming up the stairs two at a time, eager to see her. Then the steps would slow and he would take one stair at a time, heavily, and pause between each. He knew she was listening for him. Then there would be no sound. He would stand outside her door, waiting. Sometimes minutes would pass before he would knock. At first she could not bear it and would open the door, at times violently, and pull him inside. And then she would kiss him until he said, Stop, I can't breathe. At other times she would wait, sitting on the edge of the couch, with her legs jiggling up and down, her whole body tensed in anticipation. Then he would knock, three times, very slowly. She would get up and walk to the door, then pause. Who is it? she would say. And hold her breath. He would answer, A secret admirer. And she would reply, Well, then, I can't let you in; I don't like secrets and anyway I already have an admirer. For a moment there would be silence and he would say, What's his name? Then she would pause. How do you know it's a him? I go then, said Edy, quaintly, and immediately she would open the door.

ONE

I.

When Marie D'Anger saw that look in Edy Baudin's eye, she knew it was time to go home. He was sick of her.

The sound of the vacuum cleaner got louder and her mother pushed open the door with the nozzle. Won't be a minute, just get this done while I've got the chance, she said. Marie lifted her feet while her mother vacuumed the perfectly clean carpet beneath the desk. All done, I'll get out of your way now. Those few words, that was all it took, and Marie's hand started to shake. In London she'd said, *I'll get out of your way, then.* And she had. Packed her bags and left, with scarcely a murmured word between them.

He'll be home soon, her mother said from the doorway. I think we've done all we can. I suppose we can cope.

Marie looked up at her, seeing again the eyes that avoided contact, the flighty movement of the hands. Untethered. She could recall a time when her mother appeared confident about everything she said, or did. But not now. Only days after she had told Edy she would get out of his way, her mother rang. At first she said very little, chatted about the house and garden and good winter rains, and an early spring. But this was not her mother, or not the mother of recent times; she would not dare to call for a chat and so finally Marie had to ask, Is everything alright? Is there something wrong? Yes, well, it's your father. He's not too good. A stroke. And then her mother did not seem to have any other words about her. And she herself was little better. I will come home then, I was planning to anyway. She did not say that the man with the beautiful face and long dark hair and the slim boyish body had already left her, at least in his mind, and now she did not know what else to do. The change was so sudden, out of her control. Things she thought she loved, could not do without, were drained of all colour. Even the flat she had finally moved into after years of shared housing – always, it seemed, with other Australians – felt cold and empty. No longer could she sit in front of the long window that let in the winter sun and look out over a small courtyard. All she wanted to do was to go to bed and never get up. But this was not possible, she had to go to work, and when she got home in the early evening she would cook a piece of toast, or eat some cereal, and then retire to her room and creep under her duvet. It did not comfort her in the way she hoped, but there was nothing else she could think to do. She would sleep for a while, and then wake up in the early hours rehearsing endlessly, loop by loop, conversations real and imagined, that sometimes ended in brief joyous moments, but more often than not in such grief that she thought she would die. Before Edy, she would ask her friends around for a barbecue and they would sit outside, talking about the world and themselves, cooking, drinking, even when it rained, which it usually did. After Edy, she was not interested in barbecues or anything that did not involve him. They would spend most of their spare time in bed, if they were not planning the next backpacking holiday to France, or Italy, or South America. After Edy, she disappeared. And even now she did not know the limits of self, what was the shape of him, or her, where he began and ended and where he existed within her, created out of her own desire and imagination.

He was sitting on a bench outside the university library.

You are the second Australian I have met, but you have a French name, he said.

Who was the first?

He was a man, who did not interest me.

You are the first French boy I have ever met. Back home I knew, a little, an older couple who ran a restaurant.

That is the way. And now we are both in London, talking to each other.

At home they do not know how to pronounce my name. So they call me Dangerous, or sometimes Dare. That started in primary school. *We dare you to do something dangerous.* They both stuck.

She discovered he was a postgraduate student working on an interdisciplinary research project on the significance of lobbies in public buildings. It's about history and politics and architecture and design – and above all, power. I love it, he said. And you?

I'm the stereotype, she replied. A graduate diploma in communications. That's what girls are supposed to do, isn't it? Otherwise known as running away from the magazine I've been working on. For too long.

So quickly they recognised each other, it was frightening. That night, and most of the next day, they spent together in bed, getting up only to go to the toilet, or grab something to eat – an apple or pear, that did not taste as good as it looked. And between making love that felt crazy, disturbed, they talked. She told him about the country town in Australia that she loved – or, really, the house in the bush near the town – and the people in it that she had to get away from. She missed her mother and her brother. In exchange, Edy Baudin talked in ways that enchanted her. His dark eyes seemed to refract whatever light was in the room, the candle, the morning sun, the afternoon shadows. Later, Marie D'Anger could recall everything that he said. Edy talked about sound and movement and light and the countries he wanted to visit, the places he wanted to walk through and over and around. He seemed to be a young man with no beginnings. I am an adoptee, he said. The mother I know is beautiful and I love her. My father is very kind, but vague. Whenever I come into the room where he is sitting, he looks surprised, as if trying to work out who I am. A visitor? Some stray who has walked in off the street? He always seems to be waiting for me to be gone again.

Marie D'Anger, Australian to her bootstraps, thought Edy was the most beautiful man she had ever seen. She was always touching him, smelling him, nuzzling into his neck; she wanted to get under his skin.

For six years she had imagined this moment, the final return home. Now the winter sun, so bright to her eyes, flooded the desk and the papers spread out before her. Somewhere in the house she could still hear her mother's quick, jerky movements and the on, off sound of the vacuum cleaner. The window in front of her was ajar and she could hear the sound of the wind in the gum trees at the edge of the lawn. Earlier, at first light, she had been woken by the throaty, hysterical laugh of a pair of kookaburras. A little later magpies began their ritual carolling to the morning. She had loved every minute of the slow waking to what the day would bring. She thought after those years in London that she had lost this feeling forever, the anticipation of the day, a desire to get out of bed and *do* things. And she knew, now, that if she began to think about him she was in danger and the day would lose its edge and she would once again become dull and listless.

Those last few years in London she had become so bored. Travel no longer seemed to be the antidote; wherever she went to get away from *whatever* worked for an hour or two, a day at most, before she felt she was dragging around the same enervated self that did not interest her in the slightest, and certainly could be of no interest to anyone else. And then there was Edy, and everything changed. With him, the fragments of herself became connected to each other; she could draw a circle which contained all the erratic and contradictory bits and pieces of her fractured personality, so that she began to take on a coherence and purpose that had previously eluded her. She believed that Edy felt the same way about her. He, too, became sharper, more defined in her presence. He lost that amiable looseness. Like the Venn diagrams he talked about, or the more evocatively named Eulerian circle, the sets of themselves overlapped, rather than intersected. All the items remained in place and they had a name: Marie/Edy; Edy/Marie.

We can name ourselves from the outside, from above, he said. Like spacemen.

Women, she said. Or, more prosaically, you are the northern hemisphere and I am the southern and together… but remember that does not mean I am 'down under' and you are on top.

Speaking figuratively – he began to argue – but she stopped him with a kiss.

———

Yesterday she had walked down the main street of the town and felt awkward when people looked at her, as if they recognised her from somewhere but couldn't quite put their finger on it. Then their eyes focussed, perhaps remembering. Marie D'Anger, that's who she was, from that family who used to own half the cape, in the old days. Things had changed, most of the land was sold off, but they still had a big block near the coast – and they'd been there longer than most people in this part of the world. The old lady had died in the fire. There was a street named after one of her ancestors, and a park. For Marie, Euro voyeur or local identity, the town was a cliché of contemporary taste. The hardware shop (replaced by a barn in the industrial area) was now a Gifte Shoppe; where the paper shop used to be there was now an internet café; the TAB shop had disappeared but takeaway chicken was still available next door. And there were new restaurants with names like The Green Leaf which sold food to make you feel morally superior.

In London, when she first started going out with Edy, people – strangers and friends – would stare at them. This is Edy, she said. I found him at the library; isn't he beautiful? He was older than her, but only by a year. He was sophisticated, and awkward. He had read poets and philosophers that she had never heard of. He could tell jokes in four languages, three of which she did not know, including French. His smooth body was clumsy in company. Why are you staring?

she whispered to her friends. When you are with him, there is something about your eyes, they said. Alive, and dangerous, they teased. And his, too, when he is with you. As one. And he *is* beautiful, she said. Yes, they said.

The papers on her desk were riffled by the breeze. She placed a stone, shaped like a small loaf of bread, on top of them. She needed a job. *Part-time journalist required.* She took out her CV and began to select a few details. Did she know too much, or too little? She would find out. She heard the sound of a vehicle pulling into their driveway, and then the doorbell. Her mother's running footsteps. She pulled aside the curtain and saw backed up to the front door one of those special taxis, not the ambulance she expected.

Marie, Marie, it's your father. They've brought him home. Oh, dear. I hope...

In the last few weeks there had been workmen every day doing things to the house. A ramp had been built at both the back and front doors. Another from the patio to the lawn. The bathroom had been remodelled so that a shower chair could be manoeuvred into place. There were chrome handles everywhere. This was not the homecoming she had imagined.

Marie, could you come and give me a hand? Please?

Give me your hand. That's what Edy used to say. She did not understand why he changed.

Marie remained seated at her desk. She did not want to see him, not because she would be shocked, or feel sad, to see a man, her father, so altered, so different from how he was when she left to go to England. She did not want to see him because she was frightened that he would see that in this moment she was happy, exultant even, and that he was powerless. But maybe it would not be like that. When she set eyes upon him, she might feel differently. Helplessness in any form made her empathetic, brought tears to her eyes, even when she knew it was ridiculous. A three-legged cat, an arthritic dog with trainer wheels, frustrated parrots in cages, wrought the same response as the distorted, suffering bodies of starving children. Images of distressed people on television. All made her body weak with emotion. She was embarrassed by the tears that ran down her cheeks; she felt superficial and pathetic, incapable of dealing with pain that involved her personally, or distinguishing between what should move her and what should not. And yet she knew when she saw him her heart would be hard, her eyes unable to disguise her triumph.

It had not always been so. But she could still remember his words. So, you want to go to London, do you? Well, you'd better get your bags packed now, and get out of here. You don't belong in my household. I don't support anyone who chooses to leave me. Not your brother, not you. Don't interrupt. I haven't spent years bringing you up, helping you in every way possible, always thinking what was in your best interests – and you throw it in my face. Who are you planning to go with? Actually, I don't care. Just get out of my sight.

And so he threw her out of the family home. A father's love. And of course there was no financial support. Then came her birthday, just days before she was due to leave, and he suddenly changed his mind about her. You must have a party, invite all your friends around. We never miss your birthday. Reluctantly, she did so. On his insistence, she sent invitations to everyone she could think of. Why was she so foolishly obedient? And then on the day of the party, he cancelled it. He couldn't be there, he said, so she would have to call her friends and tell them not to come. Such controlled, vindictive anger. How was it possible that a parent could treat a child with such heartlessness, such ridicule? And how could she have been so weak? It was said that you have to love someone before you could hate them, but she did not believe this to be true. If you loved someone, that was it. You were both blessed. Forever. If you stopped loving, you could remember the time when you did love. You would remember all the kind feelings that went with it. It might cease, but could not turn to hate. And anyway what was it that she had done that was so terrible, unforgivable? At twenty, she wanted to start living her own life. What did he expect – that she should live under his roof, his protection (as he saw it), until she was an old woman, or until he died? Only a crazy person would think like that. And now here he was, in the next room, in a wheelchair.

She walked in and saw her mother standing with her back to the room looking out the window, then her father seated in front of her. Suddenly the chair heaved around and there he was. Dad! She moved towards him, and stopped. The face was awry, one arm hung limply. One eye drooped. But the other, uncannily, was unchanged. That single eye was the same as always. People speak of eyes blazing, and she could think of no other word to describe his. One good eye stood out in this ruined face with all the sharpness, the knowledge, the power that she had always associated with him. Now, she guessed, there was little he could do by himself. Except think. She took his good hand in hers and gave it a squeeze. It's good to see you. He grunted something in reply.

I don't mean like this, of course. I don't mean that it's good that you are in a wheelchair. It must be horrible, beyond imagining. What I mean is that it is good to see you again.

She could feel his hand withdrawing.

It's been a long time, I know, and I would have come home sooner, but you know how things happen, and I had a good job, and friends, so you just stay on, and suddenly it's years since you've been home and you don't realise it. Then when you see people again, you are surprised at how much they've changed, and you understand that time really has moved on, and everybody is older and having babies and mortgages and living, I suppose, a grown-up life.

While she rushed on, nervous and embarrassed by what seemed to her a callous disregard, he stared at her.

I'm sorry I couldn't get back for Nan's funeral. As I told you, I didn't know until it was too late. It must have been horrible for you – and of course for her. To die in a fire! And then he swung the chair around and called out something like Room! – or was it a groan that escaped? – and pointed. With a slight grunt, her mother put her weight behind the chair, and pushed.

Marie sat down in the chair by the window. Her knuckles were white. Why did she say such things?

2.

Why *have* you come back? His voice was slow, as if he had to think about the words, but clear enough. He had waited three months to ask her this question.

It was time. I had been away for too long. And I thought Mum could do with some help.

He ignored her reply, and seemed to be staring over her shoulder, out of the window and into the garden beyond.

She did not know where to look at him, the fierce good eye, or the slack one. She felt he was either too much there, too much in the room and confronting her, or not enough, scarcely there at all. What his life encompassed was simple – all or nothing, black or white – and now his body spoke the same message. Yes, she thought, that was it. Now he contained within himself the two worlds that previously were apart. In the past he had been the all – and everything beyond, outside of him, was the nothing. But no longer. Now, perhaps, he would begin to understand how others had felt in his presence. You were either with him, or against him. Slights emerged out of thin air. A tone of voice, the preference for one writer or movie over another, one person as a friend over another as an acquaintance. And even the choice and preparation of food. All were an excuse for his anger. Her mother had not withdrawn into silence; she actively, vociferously, supported all that he said, or did. Kenneth (a name that even as a child she had thought old-fashioned) was the rock her mother had foundered on, but here she had not come to grief, only relief in the solidity of the rock, its unquestioned authority.

While the children are young, you should stay at home. Go back to work when they are older. Enjoy the time with them. And she had. She was a good mother, in the way such things are measured by the world. She rose to meet every practicality, real and imagined, with a precise efficiency. Clothes, food, sport, music lessons, homework, excursions at home and abroad, not an item overlooked. Terms, places, events, people, pick-up and delivery times, all neatly marked on the calendar. What Helena did not know, or care about, was whether or not stars had souls. Nor did she know what to say to a daughter who wanted to be an explorer, or maybe a frogbuster (reports of plagues were common at the time), who did not like wearing dresses and who, for some reason, found it difficult to call her parents Mum or Dad, and so settled on nothing. Unlike her brother, Nicholas, who was such an agreeable child. Marie was a mystery she would leave to Kenneth. Perhaps he would understand her. And for a time, that was the case. Marie could talk to him about whatever came into her head, however strange or fantastical.

As she grew older, Marie learned not to interrupt the flow of her father's ideas; she realised there was really very little talking *to* him. She grew used to her silence.

Now he was sitting in his chair, in front of her. Sit down, he said suddenly, as if recalled from somewhere entirely different. I find it difficult to talk to you when you stand like that.

Like what, she thought, but sat down as requested.

What is the real reason? That man you were in love with, where is he? Edy, I think he was called. Neither a boy's name, nor a girl's. What has happened to him? Does he have a surname, or is he fashionably singular?

The fierce eye stabbed at her. Think of his weakness, look at his bad eye, the slackness of his body. Remember, he is a *fallen* tyrant. Maybe not a collapsed statue like that other one on television, but weakened, reduced, dependent in ways he must find demeaning.

Baudin. That is the name he uses.

A name he *uses*? What does that mean?

She shook her head. I do not wish to talk about my life. It's my business, to deal with as I choose.

As I thought. Running away. Again. You have no capacity for commitment, or love; if you think only of yourself, do only what you want to do, you will suffer and probably cause others to suffer.

Yes, she said, you are right about that. She wanted to say more. She wanted to say, You would know, but then she would feel childish. Instead, she turned away from him and walked out into the garden. Here she found her mother, pulling the hips off roses and putting them into a bucket.

You have the garden looking lovely, she said. And then, Why is he like this? Why does he hate?

Helena looked at her, surprised. Sweetheart, he does not hate you, or anyone. If anything, he loves too much.

So much so that he wants to destroy? You think that is love? Well, I don't – and never will…Do you think he loves you, his wife, his possession?

Helena looked puzzled. He has always let me do whatever I wanted to. I have always been in complete charge of this house. However I wanted to fill in my day was up to me. When you children were older, he encouraged me to go back to work, he thought it would be good for me. He really does think of others, you know.

You don't need him to *let* you do things, as if you are a child, she replied.

Helena put her fingers through her hair, as if making some fine adjustment to it, and looked away.

Her mother's hand reached for another overblown rose hip. Marie noticed how the skin, once unblemished, was now blotched and marked with liver spots and freckles.

I just want to say this. My father is changed physically, of course, but he is still the same man who hated his daughter leaving home and has never forgiven what he saw as my rejection of him. After Nicholas left, he focussed everything on me.

Kenneth D'Anger moved his wheelchair closer to the window. He could see his wife and daughter conversing with their hands, their voices rising and falling, but he could not hear what they were saying. And then 'Nicholas' floated across the intervening space of the garden. So they weren't talking about him at all, what a terrible husband and father he was. That would come. Rather, Marie's brother, his wife's son, was their topic of conversation. No longer his son.

There was a chain you could hang yourself from: his mother, Hetty; father, Fredric; his brother Andrew; himself; and Nicholas. His problems with Andrew began a long time ago, with Hetty's decision to marry Philip. Why she chose to was beyond his comprehension. But Andrew didn't seem to care. He remembered the first time he and his brother had decided to put lighted candles on either side of their friendly arm wrestle. They had been talking about their mother. Their faces had gone red with the strain, veins bulged in their arms and necks. Finally he had pushed Andrew's hand onto the candle, and held it there. He could still recall the smell of the flesh, the nasty blister that took weeks to disappear. Andrew was filled with all sorts of resentments: Kenneth's job, his wife, his children – and the fact that he, Kenneth, had inherited the house that had originally belonged to their maternal grandparents, and then their mother.

This was a house with the ocean as its front yard, the bush behind, and no visible neighbours. It was the house they returned to every school holiday, every university break. It was the place they imagined when overseas travelling or working. It was a haven that took on the perfection of long summers and untroubled childhoods, all painful memories erased. He knew Andrew believed that when his older brother inherited the house and some adjoining acres, he also inherited the past, *their* past, such as it was, and as the younger brother, his only rights were those of a visitor. His slice of the estate was an expensive city apartment, some shares and an industrial block on the outskirts of town. When Philip died, and long before her own death, their mother had decided, generally and unhelpfully, to leave all her property, and goods, in equal parts to her two sons. They had to work out themselves how the division would occur. And she wanted it to happen immediately. To end their bickering, Kenneth had suggested that they toss a coin – in good Australian fashion – and that whoever lost had to decide what constituted 'equal shares' and then offer the first choice to the other brother. Andrew lost and Kenneth chose the family home.

3.

Sitting staring out of the window Kenneth D'Anger felt old, not just because his body had let him down so badly, but because of his mind, or perhaps more generally, his head. It seemed to him these days there was a cloudiness that was both inside and outside his skull, like a low mist that he could not quite penetrate. Ideas would come to him, sharp for a moment or two, then disappear and he would struggle to recall them, to remember what it was he was thinking about. Even his plans for the day would come and go in this fashion. When he first started to recover from his stroke he would wake in the mornings, perhaps from some dream or another of when he was a child or a young man, and he would feel good and positive, his body whole and youthful. Then it would strike him. He would remember. An invalid, that's what he was. And he would think how frequently he had, in the past, misread the word when he came across it. In-valid. But then really they were about the same, a short shift from not strong to not true or legitimate. And so he would lie there and think about the empty pointless day ahead, full of challenges and minor embarrassments for himself and others condemned to look after him.

He raised his body a fraction in his chair and tried to get comfortable. Outside, his wife and daughter continued to gesture their way towards some understanding. Whatever it was, they were unlikely to share the information with him. He watched his daughter thread her hand through her hair and hook it momentarily behind her ear. That movement. It was as if some trick had been played upon him and he was back there, once again, in the protective light and warmth of a Greek village in early summer. Returning from England he had decided to break his trip and take a week off, all by himself, and stay at Benitses on the island of Corfu. It was not like him to make such a spur-of-the-moment decision, but he did not want to go straight home after three weeks in London. The time had been taken up with a law conference, work-related meetings with colleagues, library research, unavoidable visits to friends and distant relations. Not really interested, but he did it. Now, time for himself.

In the fresh morning air he had set off up the winding path to visit a chapel he had read about above the village. For him it was a picture-postcard landscape with a dirt path tracking through olive trees with trunks so old you felt in awe of their gnarled and determined survival. He paused and looked back down the hillside to the perfection of the bay and (of course) a fisherman upright in his caique rowing with such practised ease he too seemed to have been there for centuries. The wake of his small boat spread out far behind him in the still waters. Everywhere there was a gentleness he was unaccustomed to in Australia. When he reached the chapel he was surprised to find someone there before him; he had seen no one on his walk. He sat a little behind her on the other side of the aisle. She had on a white dress, and a veil; she had dark olive skin and wore leather sandals. He could see her feet were covered in a fine dust. In the light of the chapel, she looked golden. They emerged together, not entirely by accident. She removed her veil and ran her fingers through her dark hair which shone in the sunlight. He thought she might have been an actress on holidays.

Sitting there, he remembered that week in Benitses with a fierceness that surprised and pleased him. And yet it was the beginning of the end of how he had lived his life for the previous decade, if not all of his adult years. Chrysanthe, the golden one. He could still see her smile, her brown limbs, the intense look in her eyes. That was it, he thought. Intensity. And he came back to Australia, back to his home by the ocean, where the light was sharper, the coast bigger and wilder, the tracks prickly underfoot, the waves threatening – and everything else lulled into a benign meaninglessness. His work, his family, his friends, all kindly and well intentioned – or so he'd thought until that dreadful business with Nicholas, and Helena, and Andrew. Nicholas said he couldn't stand living with his family any longer. He meant his father. The man he couldn't disagree with about anything. He was going to live with his uncle, Andrew. If you walk out and leave, you go forever, you understand? Nicholas nodded, and left. And Andrew accepted him; more than that, welcomed him gleefully. Andrew, who had no wife or child of his own. Helena said not a word. At heart Kenneth felt an emptiness that frightened him; at first he did not know how to continue.

Then gradually the familiar patterns returned, but it was not only Nicholas that he missed. There was the golden woman he had met in the light-filled chapel in Greece. He believed that such a chance meeting could not easily be dismissed. In spite of a voice saying over and over that it was a 'holiday romance' (what a nasty idea), that in a month or a year, or five years, he could not possibly feel the same way about her – or she him – all meaning accrued around that one week on a Greek island. He felt he had glimpsed a possibility, a way of living that did not feel half alive. In that week, he felt continuously, intensely *engaged*. He did not slip into his role of onlooker, not only of other people's lives, but his own, where he *acted* Kenneth D'Anger. He felt fully present for the first time since childhood, the difference being that now some part of his consciousness was aware of the significance of the moment. The plenitude of it. Language so formal for such an experience, but he had no other words available to him. He did not know whether this was a personal failing.

4.

In her memory Edy's hands and face were always cold. They would get into bed with their clothes on and when they were warm again under the pile of blankets and duvets they would gradually remove their layers of clothes until they were both naked and clinging to each other as if their lives depended on it. They would spend hours in bed, touching each other and talking.

On these warm nights back in Australia, Marie, on going to bed, would imagine Edy's approach. The pathway to her bed was no longer clear, but she could see him, the long dark hair, the confident stride, and he would get closer and closer across roads and paddocks that belonged nowhere until he stood beside her bed. Then he would take off his boots and his jacket and slip under the single sheet that covered her. His hands would touch her face, his fingers trace the outline of her eyebrows, then her neck and breasts and belly. Impatiently, she would turn over in bed, pull the sheet over her head, and blot him out. But then slowly bits of him returned, his hands, his eyes, his lips. At these times the whole fitful night was filled with Edy. Had he so invaded her that her very self was changed, cell by cell, so that Edy *was* her, and not just imaginatively?

She remembered how he had turned towards her, one hand on her breast. With his hand there, she felt its softness, its contours, the firmness of her nipple. His eyes were dark and still. She stared into them, holding his gaze. The more she looked, the more fearful she became. There seemed to be no end to the blackness. If she blinked she might see herself reflected there. The emptiness. Who are you, Edy? she asked. What are we doing here? For a long time he said nothing. Then he said, I don't know the answer to those questions – but I think we are very different, because I do not care about either your questions, or the answers. You, on the other hand, must always break the moment we are in with words, queries, abstractions. It's not enough that we are here, our bodies touching, embracing all that we know of each other? It was her turn to stay silent. She wanted to cry out against him, the words he was saying made no sense to her. You are making this up. It is cruel. It is not how I am. You must be talking about *your* feelings. He continued, For you, I don't think it is enough. Being is insufficient. You are driven to tell everything, what you think, what you feel, to explore the reasons behind everything we do and say. She tried to put her finger to his lips, but he turned away and continued to address her. As if I'm a child, she thought. And in the process, you destroy, he said. I do not think that you can change. You rob me of the very moments that are the most intense and precious, and for that reason I cannot continue to see you. This has to end, even if it breaks both our hearts.

He sounded so formal, as if he had thought long about what he wanted to say. He had planned it all, trying to drive her away. She did not believe him. It was her heart that had stopped, she was the one who couldn't breathe. Then she took a deep breath in, out. And another in, out. If she did not keep breathing, she would die. She thought, you could not love someone so much, and yet have them leave you, to want to leave you. But that is what Edy said must happen, as if ordained by forces beyond either of them. It was not possible. Who would she be? How could she live?

In the depths of the moment her thoughts expanded; blindly, desperately, she turned to him. Listen to me, Edy, what are you hiding from? Your eyes have a wonderful light in them as if you're alive to the world. Then I look harder, or longer, and can see nothing beyond the surface. I think that deep down – or perhaps not so very deep down – you are afraid. There is silence, emptiness, which is not good. Is it because I see this void in you that you must leave? You accuse *me* of robbing *you* but I believe it's yourself that you are talking about. She thought, it is your failure to come up to the surface from behind those beautiful eyes that stops you from being in the moment, the very thing you level at me. She said, You want only a reflection of yourself, like Narcissus, and it's true that I cannot provide that. I will get out of your way then.

A week later Marie was on her way back to Australia, not knowing then that she was incapable of leaving all of Edy behind.

5.

Helena paused and looked back along the beach. The only footprints were her own, and where she had walked on the dry sand they were already beginning to disappear as the wind moved to the south-east and picked up strength. As always when alone at the beach, she was forced in upon herself. She pondered Kenneth's illness and the return of Marie and wondered what was next on the long list of events that had been imposed upon her and that had invariably rendered her powerless. Now she felt frightened, did not know where she belonged, did not know where to turn or how she could push through the chaos around her. She must find some order.

The beach ran the whole length of the bay and Helena decided to walk to the very end. It would take her an hour each way.

At the end of the bay, she turned around. The tide had come in and washed away most of the sharp, clear prints of her bare feet and the dips in the dry sand were no longer distinctive. She thought about meeting Kenneth for the first time and how, immediately, there were boundaries that made her feel safe. She could recognise, now, how the order he imposed was based on his will and his own fear of change or uncertainty. That was then. Now, she wondered what would happen. She could not get used to the idea that he might be dependent on her, even a little. And nor could he. Not yet. It was true she had prepared the house as best she could for his arrival. Objects could be strategically placed, but not people. Not her and not Marie.

———

Helena sat in the most comfortable chair on the deck. If she had opened her eyes she would have seen that the sky had changed to a brooding pink. The day had been humid and there were impressive looking clouds in the west creating a sunset that normally she would watch until the sun finally disappeared and the sky darkened, the clouds becoming ink. She was meditating, as she did now, every afternoon at this time. And first thing in the morning. Apart from clearing the mind it was, she was convinced, of great benefit to the body, especially her heart. She felt she needed that. Too many women of her age had trunks like building blocks and bottoms that forever strained against the pants that tried to contain them. And what's more, they waddled. No wonder they were called old ducks. Exercise and meditation were doing wonders for her. She still moved like a young woman. That's how she pictured herself even though she knew it wasn't true. Not entirely. There were moments when she felt she was discovering a self that might have existed if she had never met Kenneth. And then she thought, how is that possible? To erase years to try to recover someone who had never existed?

The meditation she engaged in did not belong to any particular school, or, as she thought of it, brand. She had been to a couple of introductory lectures from different teachers, which were free, and then decided she could work it out for herself. By focussing on her breathing she could empty her mind of thought and her body of self-consciousness and enter a realm that could only be described as transcendent. Body and mind were at one. Free, unattached, unfettered.

Now she could feel a cooling wind from the south-west and she entered into its rhythm and the sounds of the gum trees that surrounded her. Their eucalyptus scents became hers as she sloughed off the remnants of her body and entered a realm of pure thought, pure feeling, a perfect abstraction tainted by nothing personal or material. She was free of Kenneth, Marie, her old self. And then through a tunnel of remembered light a figure walked towards her. It looked familiar; he looked familiar. The slight sideways movement of the head, the walk imperfectly coordinated. He came closer and she could discern his features. Of course, who else would visit at this moment? Kenneth referred to him as the prodigal son, but he was not that. Nicholas was not lavish, wasteful, he would not return. The wastefulness had been all on Kenneth's side. In Helena's experience fathers were more likely to be prodigal with whatever it was they had to offer. What word would you use for someone who lavished everything on themselves? Self-prodigality?

She realised she had, so quickly, lost the space of perfection and the world had entered with its own narrative running through her mind and body. The loss of Nicholas.

Sometimes late at night, if she had not meditated at her usual time, she would sit with her eyes open and stare at a most beautiful vase she had received as a gift. The card accompanying it contained the lines

being as white as jade
as thin as paper
as clear as glass
sweet sounding as a chime

When she sat and stared at it, unblinking, she slowly merged with the vase and became as white as, as thin as, as clear as. Perfect.

TWO

Illogical preference.

I.

For weeks now, Kenneth had noticed a change in Helena. She seemed quieter, more inward, less inclined to make predictable observations and polite conversation. The very qualities that had made her easy to live with if you ignored her, but also infuriated him. Sometimes he wanted to shake her and say: Is there anything you *really* believe in? Anything you *really* feel? He wanted to explain to her that because she lacked the stamp of individuality – idiosyncrasy even – he felt unrecognised. He was some generic figure easily replaced by any other grumpy, dictatorial male. Yes. He could say he had always known what he was like but now was beginning to question his ready acceptance of that self. And there were further questions about the past, which he had consciously tried to resist – partly because it was what old people were expected to do. Avoid the present.

Become querulous and repetitive. But now it seemed he had little choice. Memories forced their way upon him. Chrys. Nicholas. Marie. Like pointed weapons intended to hurt him. And, even worse, a growing conviction that he needed to talk to Helena. Helena. He suspected she felt sorry for him because of his physical condition. It was likely she also felt sorry for herself, having her own life curtailed and controlled by all the demands that his circumstances placed upon her. Not that she was obliged to. He would have paid someone to come in and do the things she did for him. He was angry about his condition, about fate, but he had no sense of shame about the daily betrayals of his body. It was no more than what many women, and some men, did for babies, and that's what he had become. He had returned to the incompetencies of childhood. But the more his body let him down, the more he felt his mind could compensate. He read more – anything he could get his hands on, but especially history and biographies. More of the past. But he couldn't stay there. Not every hour of every day. It was too much to expect.

2.

Marie had started to keep a diary. In it, there were numerous entries about the nature of relationships between men and women, what drives them to seek each other out, why one particular man or woman would attract the other. The stuff of every second blog, sitcom, documentary posing as science, newspaper report, talkback radio program, and a plethora of websites: all knew the answers. Somehow none of their comments or advice seemed to apply to her and she thought of Miles – the geologist-turned-teacher she had recently met – and how he was such a suitable man, but she did not love him – or should she say no more than that the thought, or reality, of him did not produce palpitations of the heart? And she thought of Edy, so unsuitable in so many ways, and yet it was he who she would rush to see, travelling miles on the underground, walking through darkened streets in appalling weather, feeling a tightening in her chest the closer she got to him. This was, supposedly, how adolescents behaved, but she had been happy, ecstatic even, to discover those feelings in herself. She *wanted* the madness of it all, the crazy, overwhelming, irresponsibility of passion. The reality, however, was in its demise. He was now no more part of her lived life than a rock star pinned up in a teenager's bedroom. But that was not what she wanted. I am not a grown-up person, she thought.

Did this mean there was an inevitability about Miles, because she was no longer an adolescent? He was certainly not just 'anyone'. In the short time she had known him what they had exchanged felt important. As if they had disposed of the preamble to a friendship and immediately become involved in ways deeply personal and familiar. She recognised that this, too, was how she had come to know Edy. Now it was Miles and she wondered about the interchangeability of lovers. She shivered when she thought of it: the sense that somehow they were already known to each other. Or was he another of her creations, emerging from her own needs? When she was with him, this did not seem to be true. She and Miles talked the same language about so many things. Importantly, they could share the unspoken, a glance that suggested they were in agreement, they understood each other without the need for words or comment. And, what's more, he was good-looking. What was lacking, which surprised her, was physical passion, although she tried. They both did. Sex was comfortable, pleasant, but not driven. Was it possible to outgrow those feelings? Was it a stage? Was it something she could only experience with Edy?

The contradictions and complications infuriated her. She had been surprised to learn (from a weekend magazine) that over fifty percent of marriages in India were still 'arranged', presumably by the parents or other relatives. And most of these relationships persisted with, apparently, acceptance – even happiness. Such arrangements, made by interested second parties, could never involve the suspension of judgement that occurs when one is first in love. She had read somewhere that four years was about the longest such feelings could last, about the time it took for a child to achieve a small degree of independence. So it all came back to the survival of the species, one way or another. She, however, preferred to hold onto the grudging acknowledgement of Nietzsche: There is always some madness in love. But there is also always some reason in madness. She felt she had her reasons with Edy, and they were not all superficial. She was not some flaky teenager, after all. Mad, maybe. She wrote out a line from Wordsworth. *We have given our hearts away.* But not to Miles.

Nevertheless, he was the current reality of her love life, a phrase she despised, but often had foisted upon her. What to do with him? She was not absolutely sure that it was her choice; his feelings for her were, at least, muted. Did he, too, have a secret love, someone he could not forget? She did not think his heart beat wildly at the sight of her, or that his blood rushed to his extremities when he thought about her. Perhaps this is how responsible adults felt about each other. They weighed things up; they considered the pros and cons.

They did not measure the depth of their relationship by the length of a trail of clothes strewn across the floor. You did not choose who you fell in love with.

She heard her mother's voice, Marie, isn't it time you left for work? She would be late again for her part-time job at the local newspaper. They had discovered that she did not know too much.

3.

Through friends of friends she had finally run him down – a flat on the edge of the city that was predictable in its arty, male messiness. She had surprised him but it was late in the day, so he was not in bed but rather preparing what was probably breakfast and lunch combined. He immediately offered to fix her something as well, which she accepted.

You're impossible, Nicholas. You never ring; you don't email; you certainly don't visit. I didn't know how to get hold of you. It took me ages to track you down.

So? Why would I? Who cares? This is the first time you've been to visit me.

That's true. Nevertheless it's quite a trek and, as I said, you're not easy to find. And I did live in England for six years, a little distance away. And this is only the second time I've been up to the city since coming home. So. There *are* ways of keeping in contact, you know. And what if something happened, what if there was an emergency?

Really? Here – try this, he said. It's got everything in it.

He was right, she needed two hands to deal with a roll stuffed with marinated eggplant, cold meat, salad, pickled cucumber and red capsicum.

This is delicious.

I'm known for my rolls, he said, between mouthfuls. Why have you come to visit?

To see you, of course. And then she told him of seeing their father again after his stroke and how much he'd changed physically, but otherwise seemed just the same: impossible. And how hard she found living at home again.

What did you expect? Why do you think I left, years ago? That's him, said Nicholas. Well, the pair of them. And you, he said, shaking his head.

Don't you think you should see him? Now that he is not well?

Look, he forced me out, much the same way he did you. An obsessive bully. And Mum, well, she just went along with it, as usual. Never question the boss. You can't do that; be so rejecting and think someone, a child, will just forgive and forget. Has he said he wants to see me?...No, of course not.

You know he would never say that; but it doesn't mean he doesn't want to see you. And I know Mum misses you. A great deal, I think.

Yeah, well. I think it's time they grew up. Especially him. He believes his father abandoned him and his mother rejected him – in spite of all the evidence to the contrary – and he has now done the same thing to his children. Knowingly. And of course he thinks his only brother, Andrew, was part of a plot against him, stealing away his child. If it weren't for Andrew, I would have ended up on the streets. There is no way of dealing with that stuff. The thing is, Marie, I've finished with them.

Can you really say that?

Yep. Those bonds have gone, they can't be recovered, and I don't really care. I'm happy enough doing what I do. I don't feel like I'm an emotional, psychological mess because of their behaviour – but maybe I'm not the best judge of that. I don't even feel angry with them. They are like people I used to know a long time ago.

But it's not *such* a long time, she said, her cheeks flushed.

Nicholas seemed unperturbed. He shook his head. Nup. I honestly don't care. Maybe one day it will all be important to me and I'll help make some therapist rich –

Well, interrupted Marie, if you're happy that's all that matters. So they say, but I don't understand it.

Don't worry about it. I'm glad you've come to see me. Tomorrow night there's an exhibition of my photos opening – just around the corner. Do you want to come?

Of course, I would love to. I'm staying with some friends for the rest of the week before I head back down to that madhouse. I thought I should stay there to help, but I don't know how much longer I can put up with them. Dad thinks Mum is seriously weird, and in a way he's right. Nothing seems to affect her and she just seems happy to look after an ungrateful cripple. Or, physically disabled person. Whatever. She says he is her husband and 'for better or worse' means something. Don't know about the philosophic years, I think she's just soft in the head. Actually, it's not so much what she does, it's this odd, floating unreality that surrounds her that bothers me.

Yeah, well, probably too much dope. Or some guru. I'm happy to leave you to it. Why would I want to get caught up in that lot? They are truly fucked.

Yes, I suppose. But it's not that easy. Certainly not dope, as you know.

That was a joke.

Alright. Anyway, let's talk about your photographs.

We can, but we haven't talked about you. What are you doing back here, especially what are you doing down there? Have you run away?

Do you know who you sound like? Don't bother. Sit down and I'll tell you all you want to know.

4.

Helena braced herself and pushed hard to get the wheelchair to the top of the rise, her feet slipping for a moment on the gravel path. Kenneth was quite independent on the flat sections, and of course inside the house, but with only one arm that had some strength, he needed help on slopes, especially ones like this. She was puffed out by the effort, and breathed noisily.

Thank you, he said.

Helena turned the chair around in a little clearing, so he was facing westwards towards the coast. She thought she knew why he liked to come here now: it was where you could get a glimpse of the ocean between two low-lying hills. It was a spot where his mother, Hetty, had placed a small wooden bench and she would often come up here and sit and read, or just stare at the view.

Do you want me to leave you for a while, or should I stay? She sat on the weathered garden seat next to his chair.

I would like you to stay for a little while. He turned to look at her and Helena did not know, yet again, which eye to focus on. There are some things that I think we need to talk about, or perhaps I should say *I* need to talk about.

That sounds very serious, Kenneth.

Yes, I think so. He paused. Even though it was a very long time ago, do you remember, when I came back from

London that time, I stayed in Benitses for a week?

Yes, of course. I travelled up to the city to meet you and we spent the night in that hotel. I can still recall the feeling I had that you weren't really pleased to see me. You were polite and nice, but somehow not there.

You thought that then? And didn't say anything?

Yes. And I'm not sure you've ever come back. I've got used to keeping quiet. Like Marie and Nicholas.

They looked at each other, in silence. Then Kenneth said, There is more to say, more for you to know. And he told her about meeting Chrys in the chapel, and what followed. He said he understood that because it was such a fleeting relationship it had no time to be anything but perfect in his memory. And it was a memory he returned to again and again. He told her about a note he had received, years later, and he had not replied to it.

He did not look at her. He waited. Are you angry? he asked.

What do you think, Kenneth? *Of course* I'm angry. You sound so matter-of-fact, so casual. What if it were me telling you this story?...And why didn't you reply to that note?

There was no point. There was nothing I could do with the information. End of story.

Helena turned to him, untroubled by where to look. She wanted to say, You have a lot to answer for, Kenneth. You have rejected one child, and you seem to delight in making Marie's life a misery. You insist on what you call loyalty, which is really abject dependence. And now this. What about your disloyalty, to me, and your children? The years of indifference? Instead, she said, Do you know why you behave so badly, why you are so destructive? So controlling? What are you frightened of?

What could he say to her? That ever since returning to Australia as a young child he was fearful that his mother would abandon him and his brother? That he was a clichéd expression of the child who always wanted the deserting father?

He said, I can only guess at the motives, or causes. But they're not a sufficient excuse. And reparation, I think, is impossible.

Helena stared at him and shook her head.

He shifted in his chair, trying to get comfortable.

You know, my mother seemed so casual in her mothering – as she was about most matters. But now I think Hetty was quite special in many ways, wiser and more loving. Her sense of being 'different' in the community was important to her, not merely a self-conscious display. She was genuinely independent and, I see now, courageous.

You're changing the subject, Kenneth, said Helena, sharply. You have a lot to make up. To all of us. Perhaps you could begin by contacting Nicholas – you know Marie has been to see him? And try talking to her as if she is a person. Most importantly, admit to yourself, and them, that you love them.

She could see that annoyed, impatient look on his face. She paused and added, What will come of it, who knows?

She could feel her anger rising against him, but then she took his damaged hand in hers. We are not used to this, are we? This baring of souls? There is of course much that I could say about myself, my less-than-ideal self. But I'm not sure that it would be helpful.

No. One person in the confessional at a time is quite enough. And for my penance?

I believe that is already taken care of. I'm going back to the house now. You can manage the downhill slope?

What do you think? There was a faint smile. Look at me.

He sat there and thought again about the impact of Hetty's decision to leave his father. He'd lost his sense of security and that was why he had become obsessed with control, with a desire to possess (everything, including people) – a desire that could never be met. He could see all this; he knew his weaknesses and vulnerabilities, but also the causes – and that he could do nothing about them. You didn't choose to be the person you became.

———

Busying herself in the kitchen, Helena thought, again, about that time she had visited Andrew. Things that were said. The way he had held her in his arms. And then she'd asked him whether it was possible for him to look after Nicholas, because she was so worried about what was happening to him, what might happen next.

5.

Earlier in the day, Miles had said to her, Did you know that fishing line has a memory? It wants to return to the shape it is familiar with. So, if it's wound tightly on a spool, it wants to go back there again. The best line, he said, has low memory.

But not people, she had replied, with such confidence. But was that true? Were memories that could not be erased a mark of goodness, of being the best? Was she forever wrapped around Edy?

Somewhere a door closed, her mother making sure the house was locked against the night. She sat on the edge of her bed. Edy. She is once again in that moment, on that day.

She feels his breath on her cheek and then his hand beneath her blouse. It is cold on her warm skin. He rubs her belly and then, slowly, her breasts. She breathes him in. Outside, there is a light shower, but very little wind. Through the small window she sees the heath stretching into the distance and beyond, the green hillside patched in luminous sunlight. His hand strokes the soft skin on the inside of her thighs. She shivers, and waits. She can make out a stooped figure and the rise and fall of some instrument. Edy takes her face in his hands; kiss me, he says. And she does, so eager she wants to disappear inside him. Now his hand is warm.

I wonder who used to live here. It is so hard, and lonely.

And beautiful, she says. I have heard that sometimes messages were scrawled on the walls. Gone to Australia.

They make their way up the steep slope. There are no trees in sight and then there is a man with a border collie and nine sheep. She thinks they must be his pets. And further on, another man, the rise and fall, cutting peat, with a small donkey cart nearby.

I think I am in fairyland. None of this is real. And she smiles at him, her twin.

It is to them, he says. And tomorrow we must go back to Dublin to catch the ferry. Do you think London is more real?

I don't know, she says. Does it matter? Kiss me again.

6.

Kenneth knew it was himself that he was remembering, but it still felt as if he were watching a home movie, stilted and not always in focus. It was a boarders' weekend, so Friday was a holiday. The train south from the city did not leave until the middle of the afternoon, so he had hours to spend at school before he could set off. There were only three other boys lurking around, lost, in spite of trying to look purposeful. They were worse off than he was, because they were not filling in time; they had nowhere to go, no one wanted them for the weekend. No parents or relations had arrived to bundle them into cars and take them away. Two of the boys were Asian, from that mysterious place called *overseas*. They hung around together, saying very little to anyone, including, Kenneth thought, to each other. He wasn't sure of their names. The third boy who was not going anywhere was seriously misfitted to most of society. Sean. He lived in the city, but his mother had sent him to board, presumably in the hope of recasting him for the world. Somehow he managed always to look untidy, even in a uniform. There would be buttons undone on his shirt – which was never properly tucked into his shorts – and his tie was always loose. He had fair skin and his face was invariably flushed, from exertion, or embarrassment or anger. Everyone knew how quickly he lost his temper, and so he was regularly teased, provoked, harassed, until it happened and he would throw a wild punch at someone and he would end up in trouble with the masters. He had no capacity for subtle, underhand revenge, unlike almost every other boarder that Kenneth knew. On this morning the four of them were wandering around the empty schoolyards. Sean had asked him whether he wanted to play handball against a classroom wall, but he said he didn't have time. One of the house masters would have been on duty, probably shut up in his room somewhere, reading, or doing whatever masters did when there were no boys around. You weren't allowed back in the dormitories after breakfast, but he'd left a book behind in his bedside locker and he wanted it for the train journey, so he'd gone upstairs, secretively, to retrieve it. Walking past the bathrooms on his way out, he'd heard a low noise, maybe voices, and so he decided to open the door and investigate. He did so very quietly. Beyond the urinal a cubicle door was open and standing there, looking at each other, were the two Asian boys. Their shorts were undone and in their hands were their penises, erect. He turned around straight away and hurried out, banging the door behind him.

That afternoon, he went into the city to catch the train. His mind kept returning to the two boys, their faces expressionless, looking at him, their penises, their cocks, large in their hands. It puzzled him. He sat there, by himself in his seat, no one else had chosen to sit next to him; he felt self-conscious in his uniform, although further down the carriage there was a girl from another private school who, he guessed, was also a boarder going home for the weekend. He saw she had taken her hat off, and shortly afterwards he removed his cap in what he hoped looked like a casual, accidental move, even though he was sure no one was looking at him. Then he loosened his tie, just a little. He took out his book and started to read, but kept getting distracted by the girl, who was pretty and had long dark hair. She was older than him and would, of course, not look his way. The clickety movement of the train had given him a headache, or perhaps it was from trying to read and focus on the small print. He put his book away and stared out of the window and, secretly, at the girl. He watched her as she got out of the train at the station before his. He liked the look of her slim calves beneath the skirt, which he guessed she'd hitched up when she left the school grounds, and the neatness of her stockings. He noticed her shoes were scuffed, not brightly polished as he'd expected. When he got there, he hoped his mother would be at the station to meet him, so he wouldn't have to walk in the near dark. His bag wasn't really heavy, but the night was starting to get cold. He thought again of the two boys and the surprise of their cocks, their faces. For a moment he squeezed his eyes tightly shut.

As the train slowed down, he stood up, looking out of the window at the lights and the few people standing around. There she was. He opened the door and stepped out before the train had stopped. He'd seen older men do this; they took a neat step forward and walked swiftly away from the carriage. It seemed grown-up and sophisticated. He stepped out and lost his balance because the train was going too fast and his bag made him clumsy. He staggered and fell forward, grazing his arms. Then his mother was at his side, helping him up like a child. His eyes smarted with the sting. Sweetheart, are you alright? Why did you do that? He couldn't answer her. He picked up his bag and walked towards the exit, his mother following and still asking him questions. He was glad Andrew was not with her. Then he thought of the girl, and kicked at the gravel on the path.

That evening after dinner, she stood by the fire, talking, with a glass of wine in her hand. He thought she looked beautiful with the light shining on her hair. Andrew wanted to show him a new electric train set he'd been given for his birthday, but he was not interested. At fourteen, he'd outgrown trains. Then the front doorbell rang and she rushed to answer it.

That'll be Philip, Andrew said.

Who's he?

Mum's new friend. He's nice.

7.

Helena had been working in the garden, with Kenneth sitting nearby in his wheelchair, reading. Without looking up, she said, I remember my mother cutting off a piece of my hair and handing it to me. I threw it into the fire and it singed and smelt. It frightened me because I could see how easily I could be burnt into nothing, become nothing but air and smoke. All my life I have been scared of disappearing, but now that has changed.

Kenneth looked at her, genuinely puzzled.

What do you mean? Have you found God, or has your doctor finally put you on the right drugs?

You trust nothing outside of yourself, do you Kenneth? I don't hold out a lot of hope for you. No, what has changed me is a group I go to at our local church.

Ah, I see.

I haven't told you about it because I knew you would just make fun of me, and I couldn't be bothered listening to that.

What do they talk about, this group?

I'm not going to discuss it with you, but I suppose you could say the man whose thinking we are studying was a mystic who anticipated the way the world would change, that all the ways in which people are separated and divided would disappear – and technological change is part of it, like the way the internet allows people throughout the world to connect with each other.

Really? So you look around the world and everywhere you see peace and unity – and that is why you are so happy these days? He did not give voice to the fear underlying his words: that she was happy because he was so diminished and dependent.

Helena, on her hands and knees, paused and sat back looking into the dark earth she was turning with the small garden fork. She was preparing the ground for bulbs and she could already imagine the colourful designs she would achieve with the pattern of her planting. But now, through her reading and thinking, the plants in the garden meant more than conventional notions of fertility, or aesthetics. It was a social network she was engaged in. Behind the brilliant array of daffodils, and jonquils, and even tulips, she would plant delphiniums with their awesome blue. Such authoritative, stately plants, she thought, well bred, nicely spoken, always well turned out. At the very front of the bed, she would plant ranunculi and anemones – a bit apologetic and plebeian was how she would classify them, easily distracted. Rather like her own mother, she thought, who could focus only when she gardened, often talking to her plants. In a bed of their own would be a clump of Iceland poppies, those blowsy, whimsical flowers strangely resistant to the wind, in spite of their long stems. And daffodils, distant but sure of themselves.

As for Kenneth and his narrow view of the world, he would not begin to understand her new-found pleasure in the garden, her sense that everything was connected. He seemed to *accuse* her of being happy. He would have said she had *turned* on him because she wasn't in the same state of mind that he was.

She started to tell him about her reading, about Teilhard de Chardin, a Frenchman, a geologist and a priest, not a guru, and long dead, who believed in the evolution of consciousness, an Omega point. She said, He was a man who believed that when humanity reached that stage it would mark the end of personal ambition and desire. And that our communication with each other flows from our communion with God and our communion with the earth.

He raised his hand, interrupting her. You have obviously thought about the matter, very deeply, but stay with the bulbs, he said. They do look pretty when they flower.

8.

He lay facedown in the sand, his head resting on his arms. The sun warm on his back and legs, sinking into him. If he turned one way he could see Philip and his mother lying together, and further away Andrew by her side. Andrew was lying where he had wanted to put his towel; he didn't want to be next to Philip. Or Andrew. He had placed his towel so that it was not in line with the others. He noticed a glance between his mother and Philip and knew what it meant. When he turned over to lie on his back, he saw that his mother had slipped the straps of her bathers off her shoulders so the sides of her breasts were showing. She was being silly and he felt embarrassed for her, and then for himself. He needed to go for a swim. He stood up and walked awkwardly towards the water hoping no one would notice. Andrew followed him in with a tennis ball that he wanted to throw, skidding it off the small waves so you had to jump and catch it, like a slips fielder in cricket. Kenneth played this game for a while, and then got sick of it, and threw the ball fast and wide, way past where Andrew was standing, so his brother had to swim out and retrieve it. He stood in the water and watched his mother and Philip; they had moved their towels closer together and were talking, with their faces nearly touching. Then Andrew ran out of the water with his hands cupped together and splashed them. They laughed and then Philip jumped up and started to wrestle with him, and Hetty joined in. Kenneth stayed where he was, waist deep in the water and shivering.

He remembered that day. It was the first time he had seen, clearly, that there were three of them and one of him. From then on it didn't seem to matter what he said, his mother was not really listening. The words she said hadn't changed. She asked him about school, his friends, sport, what he did in his spare time. He was still *sweetheart*, but he knew she didn't care enough. She was being the mother, saying and doing what she thought she needed to do. When he was at home and they went out somewhere, he was always invited – to go and visit their friends where there were children his own age, or to go on picnics, or the local show, the occasional concert, even exhibitions. Sometimes he would say yes, but most often he would stay at home by himself. Andrew always went with them. He didn't seem to notice that their mother was different. Later, Kenneth realised that she had not changed towards his brother, it was only himself that she had lost interest in. When he was much older, he wondered whether it was because he reminded her somehow of their father. Although he and Andrew looked very alike, there was no doubt that they saw things differently. He,

Kenneth, couldn't let things be, couldn't easily accept the world as it was, or appeared to be. Always he wanted change, something else, not necessarily more, but different. Safer, somehow. More organised. Andrew would smile, Don't get so bothered about everything, it's okay. But it wasn't. And Philip certainly wasn't okay. He could acknowledge later that there was nothing wrong with the man, and his mother most certainly seemed happier. It was just there wasn't anything very *right* with him. Pleasant, easygoing, that's what people would say. So, who cares? Well, obviously his mother cared, and probably Andrew. Andrew was there all the time; he hadn't been sent off to boarding school, to get him out of the way. He was the nice son, everybody liked Andrew. His mother said she couldn't afford to send both of them. If anything, she felt it was unfair to Andrew to keep him at home and send him to the local school. He, Kenneth, was the lucky one. He had all the advantages of a private school education. How often had he heard just those words? He smiled at the thought. And he didn't believe his mother couldn't afford two lots of fees. He thought she kept Andrew at home for his company, because she liked him, loved him, more than she loved her older son.

Andrew was saying, Come on, come on, you've got to come with us. It won't be any fun if you don't. It was winter and the sun was shining. So he'd gone on the picnic to the falls and wandered away from them. There was a sloping path along the edge of the creek and he'd kept climbing over the granite rocks to the top. Everywhere it was damp and slippery, and there were ferns growing that he'd never seen before. He sat on the hillside near the top and could see all the way to the coast, a thin, hazy strip of blue. It was still, and he thought anything could happen. He stayed there for a long time and thought about school, his mother and Philip and Andrew way down below with their picnic fire, and the father in Paris he would never get to know. The sun had gone behind some clouds low in the west and the rays were brilliant, expectant. He heard them calling him, so he stood up, his body stiff with sitting, and beginning to get cold. He stayed where he was, surrounded by the trees and undergrowth near the creek. He knew it was not easy to find people in the bush, unless they wanted to be found. It took them another half hour before they saw him. It was Philip who pushed through the tea-tree to his spot beside a pool of water. He had hoped it would be his mother, or maybe Andrew, but not Philip. His mother put her arm around his shoulder. We started to worry. Didn't you hear us calling you? He wanted to be rude to them, to say of course I heard you making all that noise.

On the train on his way back to school, he read his book for a few pages, and then a picture of his mother lying next to Philip came into his mind.

9.

They were walking to the theatre and it was dark when the drizzle turned to rain and Edy pulled down his beanie and hunched into his coat. Marie put up her umbrella.

Here, she said, get under.

I can't; I'm too tall and if you lift the umbrella up you will get wet. You know, I don't think we know how to walk with each other, not properly, like a couple.

We have two more blocks before we get there. You will be soaked. You hold the umbrella, and crouch down.

She slipped her arm through his and pulled herself close.

They started to walk in step, at first accidentally. Then they marched along the footpath, pushing into the wind and rain. Their stride increased.

We are stepping out in style, he said and hugged her.

This is what intimacy feels like, she said. To be close and to feel close and not to need words. Although, of course, I'm speaking, but not because I need to.

The sounds of the street were muted except for the rhythmic swish of cars on the wet road. As they walked, Marie felt her body warm as if from the inside out.

Your cheeks are flushed, he said.

She pulled up the side of his beanie and pressed her lips against his ear. I have a secret, she said.

Oh?

I'm not wearing any knickers.

You are a disgrace!

I didn't mean not to. I forgot.

You cannot forget, especially when it is cold and wet.

I'm wearing a long skirt and it's quite tight, as you can see. And warm.

I think you are making that up, to distract me, to make my heart run. To make me feel out of place. That is what ecstasy means.

Are you beside yourself? she asked, laughing.

After the play and when they returned to Marie's flat he undressed her very slowly and discovered it was true. She was a woman without underwear. He kissed her, all over her body, and she clung to him, pulling him into her.

Is it possible? she asked.

What?

To feel like this, forever?

10.

Kenneth looked at his mother, Do you mean I'll have to change my name? Are you going to be Mrs Aspinall?

No, darling, of course you don't. And I'm not sure I am going to be Mrs Aspinall. I quite like being Hetty D'Anger, even though it will shock all our friends.

It lasted twelve years, that marriage. She did become Mrs Aspinall, but afterwards, after the accident, if that's what it was, she changed her name back to D'Anger. It suited her better, he thought.

11.

As he grew older, left school, and started studying law at university, Kenneth's feelings about Philip didn't change. He knew he was being unfair, childish even, but every time he saw him, especially with his mother, there was conflict.

What you have is an *égoïsme à deux,* he said to them on more than one occasion, showing off his latest reading. Look at the way you live down here, closed off from the world, making sure nothing intrudes to upset your cosy view of each other. You're smug, the pair of you − but one day something will happen to overturn all this, and he gestured at the perfect arrangement of the room they were in, with its stylish, comfortable lounge suite, careful placement of original paintings (which he considered rather ordinary, too decorative), muted colours of the walls and carpet and the single vase of lilies, grown who-knows-where. There was nothing out of place and nothing in it that he approved of, with the exception of the open fire, which flickered away on most evenings of the year.

Philip's response was to shrug his shoulders, gesture with the upturned palm of his hand, and smile. This polite dismissal infuriated Kenneth. His mother was not so calm; he could see the anger in her eyes although she rarely said anything by way of direct reply. That would come later. Sometimes weeks later, and he could see that she had remembered what he'd said and that he had hurt her. Her critical comments were invariably very formal and controlled. She would not descend to explicit language or expressions of anger. On one occasion she had stopped him when he was talking about work to say, 'Your attitude to Philip diminishes you.' And walked away.

Eventually his visits petered out, probably about the time he started working for a firm in the city, before he headed overseas.

Not long before he got on the boat, the news came through. It was Andrew who told him. Philip was dead. He was swept off some rocks while he was fishing, or walking, no one seemed too clear. There was a huge swell running. Their mother, so shocked, retreated to some place where she did not have to talk. Immediately his feelings about Philip changed, as if some mist that had always disguised the true man had lifted from his eyes. Like Saul, the scales had fallen and he could see clearly. Were they fish scales? he wondered. And what were they doing on your eyes in the first place? What surprised him then, and now, was that he knew how unreasonable he'd been, and yet he had persisted. He was like an addict with part of his brain telling him one thing, and yet doing another. Now he was free. He could see the man for what he was, not so much an intruder as an object collected by his mother to be displayed in the comfortable sitting room of her house for him and Andrew and other visitors to admire. He could almost feel sorry for him.

When he next saw Hetty, before the funeral, he, like everyone else, noticed the change in her, the effort it took to talk to others, to stay in control and to be polite. He knew – and perhaps Andrew did too – that for her, her older son was a special case. Beneath the words there was another message for him. He was responsible. It was simple: he had killed the man she loved. It was obvious to him that this was what she thought, although never spoken aloud. It was his constant criticism, implied and explicit. It was his years of undermining the man and their relationship at every opportunity. He would not forgive her for that accusation. How could a boy, and then a young man, possibly be at fault in such an egregious fashion that a mature man would be destroyed? He could see through her, could see that at heart she felt guilty about this man, about her relationship with him and how it had affected her sons, or at least himself. She had failed in her brief marriage to their father, Fredric, the Frenchman she'd met in Paris, and she had carried that sense of failure with her. That much was clear. Her second marriage was no more than pretence, not one that she could look at honestly, admit to its emptiness. Instead she tried harder, pretended more fiercely, and it was up to him, Kenneth, to tell her – and Philip – how things really were, to try to force them to face up to the game they were playing, not just with each other, but with everyone who knew them, including her elder son. When he boarded the boat, there were tears in her eyes. All he could think of were the lines from the play, *Othello*, that he had studied so hard for his Leaving exam, years ago. He could have quoted them to her.

O, devil, devil!
If that the earth could teem with woman's tears,
Each drop she falls would prove a crocodile.
Out of my sight!

He had been told that there was a story behind these lines – that crocodiles cry for the victims they are eating. He could believe it. And he wanted her out of his sight.

12.

They made their way along the pathway through the trees to the rise above his mother's house, which had been empty since her death. She'd left it to Marie in her will, but as yet the girl had shown no interest in moving there. Probably too comfortable where she was. With Helena's help he could manoeuvre to a point where her two gardens – the wild and the cultivated – were clearly visible.

This was only the second time he had been there since his misfortune, if that's what it was. He stared at the scene below. Those gardens, he thought, so typical.

No. I don't want to be here. Turn me around and let's go back.

Why? Helena asked. We've just got here and the garden is looking lovely. There's so much in flower, even at this distance.

I said I wanted to go back.

She remained silent until they arrived at the house. And then: Why do you think your mother left her cottage that day? She wasn't the sort to panic, and it wasn't her first experience of fire.

I have no idea. She was old and becoming foolish.

13

He felt invaded by memories. His mother's cottage wouldn't stay away; or was it Hetty? He recalled the time, years ago, when he made his way slowly up the hill to visit her. It was a day to savour. After the violence of the night, fierce wind and rain, trees lashing and groaning against the window, the morning was a relief. It was perfectly still and the sun shone with a sparkling newness on the wet, shiny leaves of the flowers, the low bushes, and the scraggly trees. Open patches of ground steamed under the warmth. He imagined green shoots from seeds beneath the ground uncurling like a time-lapse photograph. In places, new-grown bracken broke the surface like a delicate wrist. Where the ground was soft and damp he could see the paw prints of kangaroos and the fresh skittering of sand where they had turned sharply, probably in panic at his presence. He had not seen or heard them.

His progress was slow not only because the morning was a joy. He did not know exactly what he wanted to say to his mother, or how she would react. His last conversation with her had not ended pleasantly. He had wanted to know more about his father, and not for the first time. Hetty had always talked in what he considered riddles. Fredric was exotic, beautiful, charming, archetypally Parisian. Paris itself was beyond compare, but she always felt she was a visitor there, even after the birth of her two children. And whether it was her projection or not, she felt Fredric was also a visitor, in their own household. Nothing, not even marriage and a family, seemed to anchor him. He was elusive, without a core of self that she could hold onto – not cling to, mind you. He was playful, amusing, but in the end she felt she was dallying in Paris with a boy-husband who failed to provide the connectedness she sought. Perhaps the sense of belonging she was after could exist only in Australia, in the place where she was born, and so she had returned. All this Kenneth could follow, more or less. But there were always vague references to her – or was it Fredric's? – 'true love'. At first he thought she was referring to Paris, or the south-west of Australia, but she would just shake her head, saying no, he would not understand. Place was one thing, but people were another. Nevertheless they could not be separated, they were like twins; one was meaningless without the other. He had no idea what she meant and she refused to offer any further explanation.

Two days previously, she had mentioned for the first time the existence of Fredric's sibling, Henri. The more Hetty had talked, the more involved – even, he would say, excited – she became. It was when his mother had said that it was Henri she missed most of all that he had become agitated. What are you talking about? Why haven't you mentioned him before? It embarrassed him to think about it now, but he had become abusive and yelled at her. Why, a man of late middle age, he should have become upset by what she said surprised him. More. It appalled him that he too might be caught up in a desire for *closure*, that shallow, foolish word bandied about publicly, privately, as if it was the common man's – and woman's – holy grail. If only they had *closure* their lives would be complete, at last they could be happy. Usually closure had a price attached to it, a large sum of money, but sometimes the price included knowledge. Who committed the crime? Why? How did they die? Where were they buried? Who is my father? What difference did it make? You woke in the morning the same person who went to sleep the night before. Did none of them realise this? Those suffering from a lack of *closure* invariably wanted to *move on*. Where did they think they were going to move to? The next street, next suburb, next lover, next job? The next victim? Those responsible for the disappearance of heaven and hell, purgatory – and even limbo, that fascinating location – had a lot to answer for. Ultimately, people had nowhere to go. There was no endgame. What they wanted was closure from themselves. He could have told them this, in the same way that he told his mother what he thought of her abandonment of his father. The father he had never known. She had bolted, he said, without any consideration for anyone but herself. Left him fatherless. And then he was confronted with Henri.

What would she say now? Something to damage him further?

14.

There was a time when Marie could talk to her father, before she grew up. Moments of playfulness.

Block your ears, she said to him. I want to see if you can hear through your mouth. And he did, or at least pretended to. Yes, he said. You have made a wonderful discovery, Marie: inside my mouth is a secret ear that can hear things that my outside ears cannot. I think it's the sound of the universe, the music of the world, that I can hear. And do you know, he said, that some animals can hear sounds that we can't? And he proceeded to tell her about Francis Galton and his invention of the dog whistle, a secret sound that could only be heard by dogs and cats, but not – *ever* – to be used when they were together in the same room, otherwise a fight would break out and the only sounds you would hear would be the dreadful screech of the cat and the howl of the dog when its eyes were gouged. As for the ultrasonic hearing of bats, he said, it is like a radar, but the sound they emit is so loud they would go deaf if they heard it at full pitch. The sound they hear is different from the one they send out. And he told her about dolphin voices – and whales that could hear each other from a distance of hundreds of kilometres – and how these sea creatures could find their way in the dark. Why don't we practice, he said, this secret, silent language and then we would no longer need to turn the lights on at night and we could talk to each other without anyone else hearing?

Yes, she said. Yes. Let's do that.

15.

Was there no end to the ways in which she had ruined his life? All those years at boarding school, loving and hating her, and Andrew. Hating Philip. Then the women. He didn't love or hate them, except for those few days in Benitses, but he had certainly learnt to dislike them, or perhaps distrust was the better word. He wanted to love, he knew that. But Hetty, and the life she lived, had taught him never to get too involved. He thought of those months, years, in the school dormitory after Philip, so distressed he would be awake half the night, crying. It was then he imagined his father who really loved him coming to school saying that he was taking his son with him. Later, when he was grown up, supposedly, and when he thought about it rationally, he could not work out why he felt so passionately. Now, grown old, he thought he knew. Of course Hetty and Fredric were the biological parents of their sons. But there were divisions. She had not loved his father, or his father's child, Kenneth. That's how he saw himself. Linked to the absent father. He had to belong to at least one parent, but how could you, when that parent had disappeared? He had connected himself to an idea empty of substance. Andrew was her child, connected to his mother. There were two opposing pairs, mother and son, father and son, but there was no father, not even a cardboard cut-out, so he had to be both father and son. And he'd failed. He couldn't be two people. There was no balance or equivalence. He knew this to be true, in spite of what people said about mothers and eldest sons. All his life he had striven for equilibrium, but it had been too much; he was not up to the task. Then she became besotted with this stranger, this innocuous, colourless man, Philip. It was far too late for a father, and anyway, what could you do with a stranger, an imposter? Hetty, he knew, had blighted his life and, late as it was, she needed to confess that she had been an errant mother. Where his life would go from here, he had no idea.

He knocked at the door. The very least she could do was own up.

She had let him in with her usual charm, expressing her pleasure in seeing him. He explained briefly, and forcefully, why he had come. Hetty remained silent for so long he thought there was something wrong with her.

You might think me unreasonable, he said, but until I hear from your lips that you are responsible for what has become of me, I can't stop.

Hetty shook her head, slowly. For such an old woman, she still moved with apparent ease, and her face, though firmly set, lacked the myriad lines you would expect. Yet her dark eyes looked troubled and far away.

Of course I loved you, she said. You, and Andrew – and, later, Philip. And, for a time, Fredric – until I realised he didn't love me, not in the way I loved him. He flirted with love, and fatherhood, and life. Henri was the strong one, the one with real passion. I left Paris not so much for myself as for you children. Fredric was not ever going to be a father except in those moments when he could display you, show off his fatherhood, his two boys, until the next distraction came along and he would be off in pursuit. Whether it was other women, entertainment, drinking parties, drugs, gambling. Yes, he was into drugs as well. One way or another, he was never there.

She paused, again for a long time. He did not interrupt.

Henri wanted me to stay, of course. Said we could set up house together, and look after you two boys, bring you up as smart, sophisticated Parisians. I had enough money to get by. Perhaps that is what should have happened, but at the time it didn't seem quite right to me. Then I believed it was important for boys to have a father. Back here there were at least family members who could take an interest in you – my parents and my brothers. Or that's what I thought, but they didn't approve of me. I shouldn't have been surprised, but I was. And hurt, of course. And I even thought I might meet some nice Australian, in spite of two children.

You see, Kenneth, decisions were not made without concern for your interests, nor were they made without love. So I cannot take away whatever pain or rejection you feel. Apart from the fact of your existence, there is no apology I can make that would mean anything – not to me, not to you. I can't give expression to a form of words that I don't believe, in the hope that it might alleviate whatever suffering it is that you are blaming me for.

He raised both his hands, as if in supplication.

No, I'm almost finished. I'm not responsible for the adult that you have become. For the mistakes, or failures, or deficiencies that you see in your life, or yourself. Your demand is unreasonable, but also meaningless. Haven't you thought about this for long enough? Too long?

When she stopped he realised that her voice had become strained, exhausted. In the space of a few minutes her face had become drawn, the skin beneath her eyes darkened. He was surprised at how quickly the strong woman had been replaced by this frail-looking figure. It made no difference to him.

I think your refusal to take responsibility as a parent is not merely uncharitable, it is blind and selfish. Which, of course, you have always been. Even at your age, so advanced as to be ancient, you can only think of yourself.

Hetty moved her hand to her chest and barely whispered, You must go Kenneth. Think about your words. What are you saying? Go home, now. Leave me.

He did. He left, promising he would be back the next day.

THREE

London, 1970. Leaving home.

When Kenneth arrived in London, he visited the Royal Observatory at Greenwich. Here he observed the Standard Imperial Measurements of the British yard, Two feet, One foot, Six inches and Three inches. The sight of these measurements laid out before him gave great comfort. He felt he had arrived at the true centre of his world; here was the source – and Australia, far away, was some accidental tributary, a pale reflection. Visiting Oxford and Cambridge, and the law chambers in which he was employed, produced a similar response. Here was the real world, real university, real law, a real job – not the shadows, the smoke and mirrors that existed back home. He went further and began to believe that here, too, were real people, and so he took to the British Way of Life like a duck to water and would, he believed, remain there for the rest of his days. His previous life working in a small city for a small firm, his memories of school and university, his friends, his mother, Philip, Andrew, all belonged in the past to a different Kenneth, a self who lacked substance. Perhaps even a ludicrous self, if he dared think about it seriously. But here, and now, he learnt there were boundaries to be respected. Life was organised, secure. He felt he was becoming an authentic person. But there were two matters linked to his past that he could not easily dismiss. One was his sense of belonging to the house on the cape, the feeling and perfume of the air around it, the noise of the wind in the trees, and the sound of the ocean. His childhood. The other was the thought that across the Channel, possibly, was the presence of his father. A man who'd never kept in contact.

Kenneth had worked in London for a year when he received the first, and only, letter from his brother, Andrew. It began cheerily enough with news about how he had finished his degree, and was now trying to work out what he wanted to do with his life. Then the letter continued in slightly different ink, as if he had put it aside, and then taken it up again. It concerned Philip and how a report had finally been received about an enquiry into his death.

The coroner could establish only that Philip had drowned, but there was no way of knowing whether the death was accidental, or not. You may remember there was a big swell running that day which could easily have swept him off the rocks, but it's still a puzzle because Philip was very familiar with that part of the coast.

I know you didn't like Philip very much, but I think he was a good man and certainly there was a change in our mother after she met him and then in the years of their marriage. Sometimes, you know, happiness is a sufficient reason for a relationship. I think his death was a very sad business, especially for her. A comment she made some time ago, but not repeated, makes me think Philip may have left a note. I don't feel I can ask her about it (and I don't think she would respond if I did).

Happiness, eh? He could see the scarcely veiled criticism in the words. So Andrew, too, was blaming him for Philip's death. What did he know, feckless as he was? Not even a proper job. Chooks with a rooster in a pen could be 'happy'. Something more was required of human beings, and especially his mother.

The final section of this letter had information in it that led to an abrupt change in Kenneth's life. Later, he saw it as a turning point, the road taken and not taken, a moment that would never allow him to retrieve a previous self that for a brief time had felt so meaningful and authoritative. At times he felt he had spent the rest of his life looking for that lost person. Hetty had decided to rid herself of her quite extensive, and valuable, property. She no longer wanted her life cluttered with ownership – but she refused to say how it should be divided between the two of them. It was up to the boys to work it out. She planned to move out of the big house and into the old cottage – after she'd fixed it up – at the end of the extensive block, on a rise above a permanent creek. Kenneth didn't trust complex negotiations with his brother at such a distance and decided to return home, perhaps only for a short time.

But then he had met Helena, got a so-called temporary job, and stayed put. It was another ten years before Marie was born. There had been problems.

2.

Marie had made up her mind she would stay where she was for the time being. Her job at the grandly named *Times* had turned out a little better than she'd anticipated and she believed her mother – and perhaps her father – still needed some support. But not under the same roof.

I want to move into the cottage, to Nan's place. It's not good to have it empty – and I can be here to help whenever you want.

Of course, said Kenneth. There is no need for you to be here, anyway. I don't know why you've stayed so long. But I don't want anything disturbed over there; it must remain exactly as it is.

Including the dust and the cobwebs? I've been inside and the whole place has been taken over by spiders – and rats and mice by the look of the droppings.

You had no right to go inside without checking first with me. By all means clean it up. He pushed hard on the wheelchair and left the room before Marie could say anything about *whose* cottage it was.

I'm glad something is going to happen over there, said Helena. Kenneth has forbidden me to even open the door, so this is a change. What a strange man he has become.

I think he has always been strange. But have you noticed how much his speech has improved?

I have – and he's getting back into his usual behaviour. Not a blessing in all ways. You know he's worse since your grandmother died. Nothing I can do. Anyway, when do you want to start tidying up? Would you like me to help?

Today – and yes, I would love you to help.

That night Marie slept in her grandmother's bed. She thought the room might be full of presences, but no one appeared, and no memories of family troubled her. There were matters to do with Hetty – and all of us, she thought – that she suspected were important, but she knew nothing about them, and they were not going to announce themselves to her. She wondered for the first time whether her mother's development of some independence from her father was in some ways connected with Hetty's death. It was not only Kenneth's stroke that had shifted the balance.

She was happy that Hetty had decided to leave the house to her. Her grandmother believed that a woman was more in need of a place of her own than a man. And Nicholas had been left quite a lot of money, so there were no ill-feelings. As she drifted off to sleep, her mind was filled with flickering images. She thought she would dream of Edy, who, even in her imagining of him, made her feel she was a woman of substance. She had depth and complexity. A woman of passion. A nuanced self emerged, a self that was hidden from Miles who allowed her to exist only in broad brushstrokes. This was not how it felt in the beginning. And it was probable that she had a similar effect on him: a narrowing, a curtailing of what he might be with someone else. And yet she could not deny there was a strong bond between them. There was a calmness about Miles which she valued deeply; he did not disturb her. Her mind was too busy and it was late in the night when she finally slept.

———

Helena had said she would come over in the afternoon to resume cleaning, but Marie decided to start on her own. Last night they had managed the room she had slept in and part of the kitchen and bathroom. Every corner of the house, inside and outside, harboured a spider: she was reminded of a scene from an old movie, *Great Expectations*, where a crone's ancient, rotting wedding cake sat in the middle of the table, covered in a mass of interlocking webs. Here there was no cake, but everything in the house suggested some sort of interruption or interference. To her waking mind Hetty was a presence, her story incomplete. She knew this was largely due to her father's insistence that everything stay as it was when his mother died. Once again trying to make the world stand still. It wasn't as if there had been dishes on the sink, or the table set for a meal, but all her clothes were still in the drawers and wardrobe, her desk full of the daily business of living, and letters, and personal items. There were photographs on the mantelpiece and in albums scattered around the living room. It didn't seem to her that Hetty had in any way anticipated that walking out of the house was the last thing she would do there, or anywhere.

As she vacuumed the passageway, she noticed again the smell that they had discussed earlier coming from beneath the floorboards, probably a dead rat, or a possum. She knew there was not much she could do about it, except wait for it to disappear. The ceiling in the bathroom was a different matter: it wasn't so much a dead smell as the whiff of plaster soaked with urine. Again, rats and possums and mice would be the cause of it. She would have to get up there somehow and clean it out, and then try to block up wherever it was they were getting in. And leave some bait behind for the mice, which were impossible to exclude. She didn't like doing this: if they died in the ceiling, they'd stink for a while; but sometimes they died in the gutters from where the rainwater ran into the tanks. She wasn't sure how much arsenic you needed to swallow before you felt ill. In the areas where there were no carpets, she swept and then mopped the floors. With the windows and doors open and the help of a light easterly wind, the house began to feel less like a mausoleum. She didn't know whether mausoleums had a smell about them or not, but to her mind the past had its own peculiar odour – and this had not disappeared. She was up a ladder, wiping away two years of stains and dusty grime when Helena arrived, bringing muffins for afternoon tea.

I'm sorry I couldn't get here earlier. I had an appointment in town.

It's okay. You told me that yesterday, and anyway there's something about this process that I enjoy. Now we can do some mother and daughter bonding – over domestic work, she laughed.

Who would have thought? said Helena.

That evening Marie went over to what she now called the big house for dinner, and to help her mother with Kenneth. It was difficult to know what her father really needed. Sometimes he would brush them off, saying of course he could do it by himself. But then at other times he would appear helpless before the simplest of tasks, and ask for assistance. She suspected it was more to do with how he felt in his mind, rather than his body.

Kenneth had pressed both of them on the details of the cleanup and again stressed that he didn't want anything thrown out without his permission.

It's important to me, he said.

Yes, we know, said Helena. But you need to understand, all sorts of things are there that can only be described as junk – and it has to go. For a start there are piles of clothes, old accounts, newspapers, magazines. Surely you don't want us to hold onto –

I don't know what I want you to hold onto, interrupted Kenneth. But it's all part of her life.

Alright, we will check with you. But the house is not a museum; that's not what you want to live in, is it Marie?

Mm. I can cope with a bit of the past, she said.

Shortly after, Marie left, finding her way in the dark by torchlight on a night when there was no moon. She had meant what she said about the past, and had every intention of going through the items in her grandmother's house that might help her to get to know a woman who seemed so self-contained and yet created such conflicting emotions, at least in her father, who now seemed unable to let go of her, even wanting to protect her, or her memory, in some way. Or was it something else? She knew that the first thing she would look at were the bundles of letters – and the photographs.

3.

It began with the discovery of a long letter from Philip. She found it unbearably sad. He talked about his first meeting with Hetty and how he had fallen in love with her. It was hard to explain exactly why, which was not surprising, but he thought it had something to do with her reserve, the sense that she conveyed of knowing things, things that were important, but rarely talked about.

When I see you working in the garden, or when we walk together through the forest, I feel you are in contact with those rhythms that are so much part of nature and yet are also beyond nature. People too. Whatever it is that holds humans together, you know the sway of it.

And others see this, not just me. They feel there is something below the surface that you are aware of, and which they are reaching towards; it cannot easily be named, and yet they see it in you. They do not know what it is they are seeing, yet wish to share the unnameable and so they talk to you about all manner of things like planting seeds at the right time in the right place, or what their children are doing, what illnesses they might have, but not the relationship between their husband or wife, or what dreams or nightmares invaded their day or night. You make people feel better, as if some important part of themselves is recognised, so they feel happier, more significant in your company, enlarged in that moment, and for a short while afterwards.

Philip said that this is what she meant for him, too. But he felt he could not reciprocate. It was a peculiar form of giving, on her part, and he felt he should have been able to provide her with something of the same comfort, and solace, and again, recognition. At times he felt he was close to doing this, but then the moment changed and he was once again back with surfaces that could not be probed; if there were secrets, he had no idea how to unlock them – and so he felt theirs was a one-sided relationship where he was good only for commonplace, practical support, and ultimately she was alone. *You should find someone who is more your equal – a better match – someone you can engage with beyond the everyday matters that you and I talk about. I am like one of those anchors on a hot air balloon, tying a brilliant, glorious object to the ground...*

Marie thought it was a remarkable letter, in all its sadness, its despair, and its insight. In her eyes, Philip seemed to inhabit the very space he claimed he could not. He *must* have been a soul mate for Hetty, not a man who was *merely* pleasant and practical. But what was it, she wondered, that provoked such feelings in Philip? What was it about Hetty that made him feel this way? Feel so inadequate. She wondered about her father's response to his mother. So critical, and so undeserved, as far as she could understand. Philip's letter was headed Tuesday, but was not dated, and made no mention of anything explicitly suicidal, or self-destructive. She didn't know what to make of it.

Some weeks later she discovered a brief note in the middle of a book. Perhaps it was one Hetty was reading at the time, and used to mark her place. Marie wondered whether her grandmother had stopped reading halfway through, unable to continue.

My dearest Hetty,

It is a wild day, so I must get outside and into that wildness. I'll test myself at the coast. As you'll see, the fire is set.

A frenzy of kisses,

Philip.

Marie thought she understood his need to go out in wild weather, but what was he testing at the coast? His endurance? His desire to live? His love for Hetty? And where was she that he needed to tell her what the weather was like? Perhaps she had gone up to the city and was expected home that day. The detail of the fire suggested the thoughtful, practical Philip, but there could be no doubt about his passion.

———

On the back of the photograph, in Hetty's writing, were the names Fredric and Henri. She had never heard of this brother, but the pair of them were clearly related, and dressed similarly, in shorts and a buttoned shirt. More faintly, in a different hand, was an inscription above the two names, in pencil: *To my dear Hetty from the twins (but especially H)*. Marie was deeply puzzled. Neither her father nor Hetty had ever made mention of Henri, or the fact of a twin brother. Hetty's silence, if that's what it was, surprised her. Her grandmother was one of the most open people she had ever met, sometimes to the point of embarrassment. On the other hand, her father was so guarded that part of him was inaccessible, even, she suspected, to himself. He seemed always on the lookout for the possibility that he would reveal too much about himself and so become vulnerable. For Marie the boundaries of self that he needed to protect extended beyond anything she could regard as reasonable, normal. She didn't know whether this sensitivity was indicative of an inflated ego, or the opposite. Whatever the motivation, she regarded his secretive nature as, at least, ungenerous, and more probably, misanthropic.

When she next visited the big house, her approach was direct:

Why didn't I know about a twin brother, your uncle Henri?

Kenneth was momentarily taken aback, then raised his head and looked over the top of his glasses: I did not have an uncle Henri. There was no twin brother. That is probably why you have never heard of him.

Marie took out the photograph and handed it to him. Have a look on the back as well, she said.

Kenneth glanced at it, flipping it over in his hands, then passed it back to her, shaking his head. I have no idea who this other person is.

But surely, said Marie, Hetty would have said something about a brother, especially a twin?

My father did not have a brother. When we left Paris, I was a very young child, so I have no memories of that time.

As for later, it was a period in our lives that my mother did not like talking about. And anyway, where did you find the photograph? It wasn't in any of her albums.

No. It was inside one of her books. I think Hetty liked using books for things that were important to her.

What else have you found?

Just one or two little notes, nothing that I could make much sense of, but they must have been important to Hetty. And another photograph; I think it must be one of you, or perhaps Andrew, with her – and Fredric. Next time I come over I'll bring them and show you.

Why not get them now? It will only take you a few minutes.

Alright, if that's what you want. I won't be long.

Her first discovery had been a French postcard, a photograph of an unknown woman draped in a revealing gown with one hand raised above her shoulder keeping a long, delicate shawl away from her beautiful face. She was wearing a large hat and gazing directly into the camera with an ambiguous smile. On the back was a note: *See you at 5pm*. It wasn't signed, but she recognised the handwriting: Henri's. Her other discovery was more puzzling, at first. It was a single sheet of fine notepaper, tightly folded, inside a copy of a novel by Jean Rhys that she had never heard of, *Postures*. It read, simply, *Farewell then, my lovely, lovely Hetty*. Again it was unsigned, but again the writing was unmistakable. In themselves these small discoveries meant little, but the fact that Hetty had kept them for so long suggested they were more than trivial, everyday correspondence.

When she returned and showed them to her father, he merely shrugged at the notes and gave them back to her. She wondered what he was really thinking and feeling. He looked at the photograph for a long time. It was of the three of them inside what looked like an apartment. He was being held by Hetty and fed with a bottle. His father was looking at the camera.

This is not where we lived, he said. I don't know where it was taken. But the child, that is me. Not Andrew. Perhaps my mother was pregnant with him. I will keep this photo, he said.

———

Two months later Marie woke to the sound of heavy raindrops plipping onto the roof, one then another. She had been dreaming and now as she came into full consciousness the details of the dream eluded her, but the feeling had not disappeared. She recalled sitting somewhere, maybe a corridor, and expecting something to happen, or someone to arrive. Then she realised she was hearing the sound of wind in the trees down in the valley, urgent and pressing. There was a rush of wind and the downpour struck the tin roof with such drumming and rattling she started to shiver. Within moments the gutters were overflowing; she could hear the water flooding onto the ground outside. She leapt out of bed and peered out of the window at the fierce watery mass. Such force put her on edge and she felt alone and trapped. She crossed her arms over her breasts and wanted someone to hold her.

Later in the day she resumed her search of Hetty's library. She pulled books from the shelves and flicked through them. Quite often there would be a yellowing piece of newspaper between the pages, the uneven edges revealing the section had been torn rather than cut out. They made an odd collection, ranging from world events to local news – presumably people Hetty knew. There were recipes and death notices. She turned her attention to Hetty's desk, every drawer stuffed with papers and there, in an envelope crammed with old bills, Marie found a letter which, it seemed, had never been posted. Perhaps Hetty had never intended to do anything with it, apart from write something for her own benefit. *My dearest Henri…*It was a brief, reflective account of their first meeting, apparently in Paris, and how, almost a year later, she had met, and fallen in love with Fredric – and the problems this created for both of them, but especially Henri. *If you and I had not met, there would be no Fredric in my life. And no children. I know it is hard for you: in a sense you lose a brother and also your most passionate friend. I would like things to stay the way they were, but I think now that is not possible. That does not diminish what we had, or perhaps still have. You will always be such an important part of my life, whether or not we continue to see each other in the old way. You are the most beautiful, most fascinating person I have had the good fortune to meet. This unworldly woman – still a bumpkin at heart – remains utterly intrigued, and in awe. My life has been transformed, and remains so.*

The letter ended there, abruptly, thought Marie. Unfinished and unsigned. Was it interrupted by some event, an unexpected arrival? And then she never returned to it? Or did Hetty give up trying to put into words what she wanted to say? It was too difficult. Regardless, it confirmed the significance of Henri in her grandmother's life. Whether the relationship was sexual did not seem important. It was emotional, full of desire and possessiveness in the way of lovers. Was Henri the reason for the failure of her marriage to Fredric, and for her return home with two small boys? Her father's response to the notes was dismissive, too casual, she thought. Too studied. She suspected the contents were not news to him, but there would be no way to prove such speculation.

4.

Kenneth wondered, how many more times would he walk up this hill? How many more visits would it take? As he approached the cottage, he saw a young, blonde woman, tall and attractive, leaving. One of his mother's many female visitors; it puzzled him why they would bother with such an old woman. He breathed deeply; this time he would keep calm. No more shouting at her about the mysterious Henri. Even though he now knew that Henri was *Henrietta* and obviously meant so much to her, which was beyond understanding. *He?* she'd said to him. Oh, no. *She.* He was going to try once again: this time he would be more insistent. He was more than sixty years old and did not want to die still puzzled by questions he could not answer.

He wanted her to talk to him, wanted to hear her say that what she had done was wrong, that she had provided more than a bad example. A relationship in bad faith, and that she had abandoned him – left him in that school where he was by no means the only unhappy boy. Without a father. It was the overseas students, whatever their names were, who'd discovered that boy Sean hanging from a tree near the oval. All this while his mother and Andrew and Philip had stayed here, sharing everything. What had he learnt from that? What message was there? You needed to do your duty as a parent, you couldn't just leave because you felt like it, because a child or children had become inconvenient. But that is exactly what she'd done. Left him. There. And now his children, how do you stop the rot?

She was still strong, his mother. Certainly strong enough to tell him, to admit to him, that she'd got things wrong and so his life was altered, probably beyond repair.

She looked at him, her eyes still bright. Her lips, like her hair, had thinned over the years.

Kenneth, do we really need to go through this again? Of course it was not bad faith. I loved Philip and I think – I know – he loved me. You cannot hold me responsible for your own incapacities. Your lack of trust, especially of women, is because of what is inside you.

And why is that? Why do you think it's inside me? Is it nothing to do with you?

He stood too close to her. He shouted at her. His heart beat uncomfortably.

What do you want of me, Kenneth? What do you want of yourself? Forgiveness? The part of you that's empty can't be filled by me, or any other woman.

Then he left, hurrying back through the trees. I will be back again tomorrow, he had said to her. I'll come every day. I won't stop. What would it take to make her admit her guilt? That afternoon he had crawled into bed.

He knew now that when women appeared to be kind and loving – exciting even – they could change on a whim. Women were good pretenders; deep down, they lacked substance. Helena, even when she talked of meditation, or spirituality, her connections with nature, it was all surface. There was no deep bond between the person she was and the words she uttered. Women were unable to love truly, with purity. Although he may only have glimpsed it in his own life, he remained convinced it was something he was capable of. Such love.

And then when the fire came, his mother had walked out of the house. He supposed she was expecting him. That day he had stayed home. The fire had skirted their property, their houses, but she had walked into the flames. She had left, again. He could see her night after night, and sometimes during the day, an old woman surrounded by smoke who begins to cough, and then falters, but walks on. Determined to escape, like a panicked bug in a fire, she turns the wrong way. He watches her, but his voice has no strength. He cannot warn her. His cry is hoarse and for a moment she turns her head, as if some strange noise has broken through the roar of the fire. She stands still, as if unable to decide which way to go. Then collapses, suddenly and completely, onto the dirt track. There is no movement, no sound.

5.

Marie had dressed for the occasion. She wore a tight-fitting top, and no bra. Her skirt was long and loose, her black undies with the discreet bow were skimpy. She could sense Miles' eyes on her as they walked into the stone cottage that overlooked the ocean. It was the weekend away that they had talked about and Miles had finally got around to doing something about it, not that it was his responsibility. It was his birthday and he had surprised her, saying it was a present – for both of them. Now he came up behind her and placed his hands over her breasts. She turned around and he slipped one hand down the loose elastic of her skirt into her pants, cupping the cheek of her bottom and pulling her towards him. She could already feel him growing hard against her belly.

You'd think we'd never done this before, she whispered.

Well, we haven't, not here. His voice hoarse with desire.

Do you think it's territorial?

His fingers brushed her bare breasts and her nipples hardened. She unzipped his pants, reaching for the warmth of him. He pushed her slowly backwards and they tumbled onto the bed. He reached between her legs, sliding her undies aside, touching her lips. Then as the moistness flooded into her, she felt his fingers go deep inside, urgent and gentle. She could feel the heat of him and tightened her grip; she opened her legs wider and pushed hard against him.

Get undressed, she said, and they both stripped, threw their clothes on the floor. Marie rolled on top of him, taking him again in her hand until he was straining against her and then her mouth. Stop, he said, slow down. She straddled him and eased him into her. She looked into his eyes and started to say something, but he raised his finger to her lips. Not now. He slid out from beneath her and crouched between her legs; she lay spreadeagled before him; she felt the excitement of his tongue licking her open. Marie closed her eyes and for a moment all she could see, and feel, was a smooth boyish body opening her up wider and wider. She felt his long hair falling on her thighs. She shuddered.

Fuck me, Miles. Fuck me properly.

Afterwards, they lay together looking out of the window at the softly rounded slope of the hill as it dropped to the ocean below. They talked in whispers, although there was no one within miles to hear them. When she closed her eyes again she pictured a man with a border collie, a few sheep, and in the distance, a donkey cart. The heft of peat.

What's the matter? Miles said, brushing a tear from her cheek.

Nothing, she said. Nothing at all. This is perfect.

6.

As winter settled in, Marie couldn't understand how Hetty had coped for so long by herself in this cold cottage. Every morning she got out of bed, wrapped her body in a scarf, sweater and track pants, and busied herself getting the fire going in the pot-belly stove. It was not a new model and no matter how big a piece of wood she put on last thing at night, the stove was dead by the morning. The old building had never been insulated and so leaked heat and drew the cold in until she was chilled to her bones. She'd had a load of mill ends delivered and these were a good size to put straight into the stove once the fire was going, but there was still a need to split some kindling, the next layer after the leaves and twigs she'd gathered to put on top of the scrunched up newspaper.

On most mornings she was organised with a little pile of wood in a box beside the stove, so she didn't have to venture outside to the woodheap. But not this one. Last night she was home late; it was dark and wet and cold, so now she didn't have any kindling and it was still raining. She knew it had started up about 3am because she'd been woken by the sound of the rain, at first an insistent pattering on the tin roof. And then the wind came in massive gusts that shook the whole house. Somewhere there was a gap in the cladding, or the lining, and she could feel a thin draft of cold wind on her face as she lay in bed, in her grandmother's bed. Hetty must have felt this draught, she thought, and she too must have lain awake on nights like this. Every so often there would be a roar that you could hear starting down the valley and she would lie there, her whole body tense and listening and waiting for it to strike the house. Everything rattled and shook. She could hear objects flying off the veranda, and imagined the roof lifting a little before settling back down. On edge for the next gust, she wondered whether the whole structure, the corrugated iron and timber beams, would rise up like a giant prehistoric bird and fly off into the darkness. She comforted herself with the thought that the house had stood there for nearly seventy years, and that was a lot of storms. With the onset of the fronts, one after another, she could hear the branches of the small trees near the house straining to breaking point and thrashing against the windowpanes and guttering. She knew the house was not in any immediate danger of any of the big trees falling on top of it: they were all leaning away from the coast, leaning away from the cottage, but this did not stop a surge of fear through her which mounted with the strength of the gusts, and slowly dissipated as they died away.

In the early morning she had thought again of Edy, and Miles. One man made her aware of the troubled and troubling depths within herself that she could only glimpse; the other made her feel safe and she knew that she could love him, but never feel in love. Now, she crouched by the dead stove, her hands warmed by a cup of smoky Russian Caravan tea, feeling as ragged as the scene outside her window. The wind had gone, but the rain had set in and everywhere there were small branches broken off the trees, dead twigs, and little streams of water running down the driveway forming gullies and eroding the hillside. It was at moments like these that she felt she needed a proper house to live in, one that did not make her so aware of every small shift in what was happening outside. But she knew also that feeling inseparable from the weather, tossed and confused by the night-time activity, was not something she would readily forgo. To be securely insulated from it all was to be not fully alive. She thought there was a reason why Hetty had chosen to live like this, in this challenging house, for decades and she felt she still had some way to go to discover what, exactly, that had been about.

When the rain finally stopped, the clouds began to clear and then the sun emerged. Apart from parrots racketing in the trees, everything was still and quiet and glistening.

In the early evening she received an email from Edy and her life would change forever.

FOUR

One morning, when Edy Baudin woke up in his London flat, he finally realised how much he missed Marie D'Anger. He was forgetting his fear.

Edy Baudin was driving on the wrong side of the road, but so long as he didn't have to turn too many corners, he felt safe enough. Within hours of arriving in this strange country he had hired a car and was driving south from the city. For him the oddness of the car did not end with the position of the steering wheel; on the door was the company logo. No Birds.

Mate, we don't use chicks or tarts or birds – take your pick – to promote or deliver our vehicles. We're not into that bullshit. Sign here. Gotta licence?

Edy Baudin did as he was told and pulled out into the steady flow of traffic, reminding himself to keep left. He had mapped out his journey beforehand with the help of a local road guide. All he needed was to purchase some basic camping gear and provisions before nightfall, which he did at a shopping centre in the first township he came to. He also bought a copy of *The Southwest of Western Australia: A Brief Local History*. He wanted a few days to himself before meeting Marie. They had emailed each other for weeks on end before he decided to come out to Australia. Sometime in June, he said. I don't know when exactly, I want to take my time, I want to camp along the way. It will be cold and wet in June, she said. That's okay; I'm used to being cold and wet and there will be time to discover what it is like to feel hot.

The day was cloudy, but not so cold, and there had been no rain. In the late afternoon he took a side road that led towards the coast. After ten minutes of driving he came to a cluster of houses and a couple of shops built on old sand dunes overlooking the ocean. He drove past them until the bitumen road ended in a two-wheel track that ran parallel to the beach. He came to a small picnic area, green and damp; there was a forlorn barbecue in the middle piled with old, wet ash. At its side were a few pieces of soggy wood. There was also a picnic table and benches and a parking spot for two or three cars. If he'd wanted to, he could have squeezed into the hatchback and slept there, and he could have satisfied his hunger with a selection of dry food and some fruit. But that was not what he wanted. He proceeded to set up his tent, using an extra groundsheet for protection from the damp. He put the tent fly over the top and re-tightened the guys all round. It was small but looked snug and watertight by the time he'd finished. Cosy, even. He then turned his attention to the barbecue and cleaned it out as well as he could.

Edy set out along a narrow path towards the ocean, looking for any dry twigs or pieces of wood that he could use to start a fire. The beach was further away than he thought and when he emerged from the dunes he realised how protected his camping site was: the wind in his face was strong and cold. He ran down the slope to the edge of the ocean which was grey and wild looking with white-capped waves crashing onto the shore. He walked up the beach, away from the settlement. The wind pushed him along and there was not a soul in sight. He gathered his hair out of his eyes and wished he'd brought something with him to tie it back. Edy Baudin was alone and exhilarated. When he finally turned around he discovered going back would be a lot harder. He leant into the wind, pulled his jacket more tightly around him and fastened the top buttons.

When he returned to his camp site, he almost dropped the bundle of sticks he was carrying. There was another vehicle parked next to his own, a large 4WD, and standing, staring at his tent, was a man, probably a bit younger than himself. When he spoke, Edy immediately recognised the accent.

I am sorry to intrude, but this is the only place around here you can camp without going to a caravan park. And it is now too late to drive on.

Edy shrugged his shoulders. He wanted to be by himself, but of course he had no rights to solitude in a public space.

It is not mine, he said. It belongs to everybody. He extended his hand. My name is Edy.

The new arrival looked embarrassed as he shook hands. Holger, he said.

Edy then busied himself trying to light a fire, while the other man started to take some items out of the back of his vehicle. Edy noticed there was a bed already made up.

A fire is nice, said Holger, even if you don't have anything to cook on it.

I'm going to try, said Edy.

Shall I look for some more dry wood?

Edy realised he had become somehow in charge; perhaps it was because he was there first, or simply because he was older. They were both foreigners. Yes, he said, that would be a good idea.

When Holger returned, he was carrying huge armfuls of wood, including pieces that would keep the fire burning for some time.

Edy nodded approvingly and then asked the German whether he would like a beer.

Have one of mine, said Holger. It is cold; I bought it just before I arrived at a store in the village here.

Later, the two young men sat around the fire on their folding chairs. Edy had eaten well. He had grilled some pork purchased from the supermarket, and boiled rice and vegetables. Holger said he didn't want any, he had his own food, but commented on how organised Edy was, especially when a bottle of wine was produced, and then coffee.

I have been thinking about this trip for quite a long time, said Edy. I have come prepared – he gestured towards the fireplace and the empty dishes – but also I know a little about this place. I bought a map in London and worked out the route I would follow and I have found out interesting things about the names of towns, the people who first visited this part of the world. Including one of my distant relatives. Well, one that I claim.

I think you know more than I do, said Holger. What is the name of your relative?

Nicolas Baudin. He was an explorer and a cartographer and he named some of the places around here, and elsewhere in Australia. I like to know the history of where I am. It helps me feel like I belong, just a little. He paused and added, I am hoping it will turn out the way I have planned.

Before going to bed, Holger told him about a news item that he'd heard on the car radio. Some days ago, maybe a week, a French backpacker had disappeared from a town nearby. He had been locked out of his hostel in the middle of the night, wearing only his boxers, and nobody had seen him since, even though he was very tall and distinctive looking. The police and Sea Rescue were looking for him everywhere, and his parents had come from France to make a plea on television for anyone who had any information to come forward, or, if their son for some reason was in hiding, for him to contact them so they knew he was safe.

What do you think could have happened to him? asked Edy.

It does not make any sense, said Holger. In the newspaper, it says nothing was stolen from him, from where he lived. They say he was – is – big and strong and can look after himself, but why would anyone want to harm him anyway? If he wanted to stay in the country, there are easier ways of doing it. It is a mystery, I think.

Inside his sleeping bag, Edy felt warm and protected but it took him a long time to go to sleep. For a while he read some information in his local history guide about another Frenchman, whose name, at least, had not been forgotten. He then searched through his pack for a printed page that he'd brought with him, downloaded from a Wikipedia entry.

Thomas Timothée Vasse (born 27 February 1774, presumed dead 8 June 1801) was a French sailor who was lost in the surf on the south-west coast of Australia in 1801, and presumed drowned. From Vasse's name is taken the name for the land adjacent to where the incident occurred, and also a number of geographical features in the area including Vasse River and Vasse Inlet.

Born in Dieppe, Vasse was a helmsman second class on the Naturaliste *during the 1801–04 expedition of the* Geographe *and* Naturaliste *under Nicolas Baudin, which explored much of the south-west coast of New Holland (now Western Australia). On 30 May 1801, the expedition anchored in a bay that they named Geographe Bay, and a scientific party went ashore. On the evening of 8 June, the party became stranded when a wild storm arose. Another of the ship's boats went to their rescue; all were saved apart from Thomas Vasse, who was known to be a strong swimmer.*

Edy wondered, how could this have happened? Perhaps it was Vasse who pushed the boat off from the shore and then failed to pull himself on board. And the boat couldn't turn around, or it would get swamped. Some of the reports said he was drunk. Edy had read that afterwards all sorts of stories emerged about Vasse. One account said he survived and was picked up by an American whaler, 300 miles south. He thought George Fletcher Moore's version in a diary entry in 1838 – that he read in his short history of the region – far more likely:

Some natives of that neighbourhood recollect him. They treated him kindly and fed him but he lingered on the seacoast looking for his vessel. He gradually became very thin from anxiety, exposure and poor diet. At last the natives were absent for a time on a hunting expedition and on their return they found him dead on the beach, his body much swollen.

It was said he spent every day staring out to sea, waiting for one of the boats to return. He ignored the plentiful supply of food and water all around him. Did Baudin simply desert him, because it was too hard to get him on board?

Edy put aside his notes, turned off his lamp and pulled the covers over his head. The wind had picked up even more and some time in the night it began to rain, heavily. He was glad he had two layers of material above him. He hoped it was waterproof. Apart from the excitement of travelling halfway around the world, and now lying in a tent on the edge of a vast ocean, he could not stop thinking about the missing Frenchman, not Vasse, but the man whom Holger had mentioned. Edy thought it was probable that something bad had happened to him.

And then his thoughts turned to Marie. His deliberate prolongation of the time it would take to see her again was an exquisite pleasure, but also a necessity. He was fearful of being overwhelmed by her, or rather the fact of *both* of them, a couple. He needed to ease his way into this new country, the geography of it, and the emotional territory of Edy and Marie. He could no longer understand why they had separated in the first place; there had been a rift, and a sudden departure. He could not say who he was and had rejected her. And yes, he had been frightened by the strength of his desire for her, a madness. Sometimes when he was walking he would discover that his limbs were moving in a rhythm that was Marie's. And if he kept going forward, unthinking, he would walk straight into her skin, become her, possess her and stare out through her eyes. And then he would panic. But later he wondered, why would you fear feeling too much? It was the lack of feeling, rather than its fullness, that was truly frightening. After a dozen emails and many telephone conversations, they would be back together again. For how long, he did not know – but this time in her country, not that he was really clear about what he would call *his* country. For the rest of the night he remained on the edge of sleep and wakefulness.

The next morning he boiled some water on his tiny stove, made coffee for himself and Holger, packed up his tent and the car, and headed further south. Holger said he planned to stay there a few days. He would look for work in the orchards nearby; perhaps it was time for pruning.

Later, when Edy stopped at a petrol station to refuel, he purchased a newspaper. At the bottom of the second page there was a small photograph of the missing French backpacker. The report was equally brief. A body, yet to be formally identified, had been found on a south-west beach. As far as Edy could work out, it must have been near where he had spent the previous night.

2.

Marie D'Anger lay in bed thinking of Edy Baudin. It was not yet light, but the early morning cacophony of kookaburras was probably what had woken her. Why they made such a noise before sunrise, and then ceased their throaty rumbling and calling, she had no idea. Sometimes she had difficulty recalling Edy's presence; his face would come in and out of focus and, more importantly, the nature of Edy, whatever it was that constituted him, eluded her. She could see him in a photograph, but that was all; he was like a memory of a memory. And that was what she experienced this morning as she lay there, snug in her bedclothes, with the cold air on her face. This person she no longer knew, if ever she did know him, was coming halfway round the world to see her again. Her body was tense with anticipation; she put her hands on her ribs to hold herself together.

The last few months had been strange; she felt dislocated. An email out of the blue.

For days I have been thinking of you. Make that weeks. I cannot understand why we separated, how things could change from such intensity to, apparently, very little. It makes no sense now and, presumably, made no sense then. I don't know why I said what I did. My change of heart (how can you change your heart, after all?) seemed, at the time, to be permanent and I couldn't cope with that change. I doubted everything I thought I believed in about the necessity of emotional ties: all was flimsy, insecure, some airy-fairy construct. Perhaps I was frightened of you, or of what I thought was happening to me. Now I am, overwhelmingly, back where I was before, my feelings for you, I mean. I don't think they ever went away – I think I forced them to go underground. But in that, over time, I did not succeed. I realise this message might – will, I suppose – come as a surprise, and is quite likely not welcome. You have probably changed, forgotten me, have another man in your life. But if, by fate, or chance, or simple generosity, or whatever forces are at work in these matters, you still have some feelings for me and would consider replying, my world would begin to feel less unbalanced, myself less abandoned. (I can hear you: 'Edy's talk always circles back to himself'.)

With love, but no expectations,

Edy.

She had emailed him back immediately, at length. Yes, there was another man in her life, but Edy was like a ghost that hovered on the edge of that relationship – and on the edge of so much else in her life. She often imagined him being with her when she was engaged in the simplest of everyday tasks, like shopping; she wondered what he would think about books she was reading and even conducted conversations with him, commenting on the characters and events. She spoke to him when she was driving, alone, in her car. He was there, far too much, in her conscious thoughts and in her dreams. No, she had not forgotten Edy Baudin and thought it was probable that she never would, or could. She would need to talk to Miles, the other man.

Marie knew that Edy had arrived at the airport in the city because he had phoned her. He did not know how long it would take him to drive south, camping along the way, but he did have clear instructions on how to get to her grandmother's cottage, which was slowly becoming her cottage. She did not think Edy would spend too much time in the outdoors; the weather had been unfailingly bad – or, simply, winter – with one cold front after another. It was not a time to be camping out, although she could understand his wish to be by himself for a period in this new country. She, too, wanted some time to adjust to the nearness of him, the imminence of his arrival. She could not anticipate how she would respond to seeing Edy again; she knew she desired him, the physical warmth of his body, his talk, the way the day would be enhanced by his presence. She did not know how long he would stay, but refused to dwell on this uncertainty.

The day presented her with one task that could no longer be avoided: she needed to tell Helena and Kenneth about Edy's impending visit. She wondered how, or if, her father would control his previously expressed antagonism; she experienced some wry amusement at the thought, but did not look forward to the confrontation which would eventuate, no matter how volatile or muted its expression. You would think the possessiveness of a father, in all its predictability, would finally fade into something like annoyance, or a vague sense of disappointment, but certainly not the rage or vitriol she expected from him. But in this she was proved wrong.

In the late afternoon Marie visited the big house and told her parents that Edy had arrived in the city the previous day; she was not sure when he would be at her place. Helena behaved like Helena, expressing happiness at the thought of a good friend of her daughter's coming to visit. Visitors were always welcome, especially if they came all the way from London, or was it Paris? And it was a good thing there was plenty of room for him in the cottage. But why hadn't she mentioned this earlier, that she was expecting someone, and what about that other boy, Miles, what did he think? Marie had shrugged and said Edy was an old friend, a dear friend, and people had more than one friend, didn't they? And she had warned Miles about Edy's arrival and he seemed to understand.

Kenneth was a surprise. He said almost nothing that she could recall. He had nodded a couple of times, as if in agreement with his wife, asked only how long Marie thought Edy would stay, but otherwise remained silent. And, for once, inscrutable – as if he were deliberately masking anything he might feel about this man whom he had accused her of running away from. She guessed there was little he *could* say because now this same man had come all this way to see her, and she was not running. Presumably that was a good thing, if logic prevailed, which she rather doubted when it came to her father. And of course she wondered about her own logic in encouraging Edy on his journey to Australia, his journey to see her. When you travel over days and thousands of miles, it is no small thing, not a casual gesture that is easily retrieved if circumstances don't turn out as you think they might.

With Helena's help, Kenneth eased himself into bed. He knew that soon he would not have to hold onto her to do this. Any sign of improvement lifted the darkness a little, provided moments when he began to think of himself as normal. He certainly would not stop the regular visits to the physio. He turned the bedside radio on and tuned into a concert, Verdi's *Il Trovatore*.

An hour later, when Helena joined him, he asked her to put aside her book for a while.

You've bought – and read – every self-help book from the local shop. What are you doing now? Re-reading them in case you might have missed some of that profound wisdom?

You're obviously feeling better, Kenneth. Is there something you want to talk about?

Yes, there is. It's Marie, or, more particularly, Edy. What has she told you? Why is he coming here?

That's an odd question; you know as much as I do. She was very upset when the relationship ended – and she came home in a rush. As you know. I didn't know she was still in contact with him, so this is all a surprise…What do you plan to do? Ban him from entering your daughter's house?

That's very helpful. No. She was hurt by him before, so why repeat it? I gather he's still a student?

Yes, he's doing a PhD.

You sound impressed, but that's not the point. He's older than she is; he must be nearly thirty.

Yes, so is your daughter. If he is older, it's not by much. What *is* your point?

What does he think he's doing? Marie shouldn't be wasting her time with him. And another Frenchman!

Totally unbelievable. You'd think she would have learned something about them from her grandmother.

You surprise me. You can be bigoted and bad-tempered, but this is silly. You must be able to see that you're talking about your own experience, the way you were hurt. You admit you know nothing about this man – and then proceed to make assumptions about his friendship with Marie.

It's you who knows nothing about him, Helena. This will end in tears, as it did before, and I'm powerless to stop it – as I have always been.

Helena put down her book and turned towards her husband.

You do look fierce with that one good eye, you know. More fierce than you would with two, I think. She drew him to her and felt how tense his body was.

You really are worried, aren't you? What is it about Edy that's so troubling?

I'm not sure. Maybe it *is* my own history that I'm projecting onto Marie, or maybe I'm just a dinosaur of a father who can't bear the thought of his daughter with a man. Other than Miles, I mean. I don't have a problem with him. Why doesn't she stick with him? I get the impression that Marie feels so strongly about this Edy that everything becomes unbalanced for her.

Well, we don't choose our feelings, do we? As you –

Of course passion is something to be desired, envied even, but it comes at such a cost, and I suppose I'd like her not to suffer that. She reminds me too much of my mother.

And maybe your father? Your French father? Here, turn over, Helena said, giving him a push. I'll give your back a massage, if you like.

He grunted assent, and struggled onto his side, and then his stomach.

Helena sat up and began kneading the flesh around his neck and shoulders. She said, You have spent most of your life in search of that passion, that non-existent person who is supposed to make you feel whole, what can you expect from your daughter?

Kenneth turned his head sideways, She's your daughter, too, Helena. And anyway, I've found that person you're talking about.

She dug her fingers into the soft flesh of his back, and didn't smile as he gave a little yelp.

Marie had a phone call, she said. Edy will be here tomorrow.

4.

In her grandmother's house Marie discovered one more piece of the puzzle that was Hetty. A letter with no beginning.

Hetty, you and my brother have always made me most welcome and, as you know, I love you both. There are nights when I'm alone in my room and I can hear the occasional sounds of the babies down the corridor, or the little noises you make when you get up to attend to them – and then I too can get up and come and sit with you – and in those moments I feel we are truly together. Watching you in the half-light feed little Andrew with those full breasts fills me with awe. It is so sensuous, but also a sense of the religious, or perhaps I mean the spiritual. When I see the calm set of your face I believe I am experiencing something very similar to yourself; it is such a special thing we have between us. At other times, if I think you may not have heard the children stir because you are so tired, then I go to them and, if I can settle one or the other,

I feel pleasure that I can take the burden from you for a time and that you have not been disturbed.

On other nights when I can't sleep and everything is so still and quiet, and every sound magnified, I imagine you close and warm in the embrace of Fredric, and all I can think of is being there with you. I am not jealous of my brother, I just want my share of you!

I cannot continue like this – and nor I think can you. Both of us are exhausted. I can see no way out. It will break my heart – perhaps both our hearts – but it is time for me to leave.

Forever yours (and I mean this with my whole being),
Henrietta.

Perhaps it should not have come as such a surprise. But it did. Marie realised she was holding her breath and could feel her heart beating. And then she thought, of course, even though she could not think why. Why it would have to be a woman. She could only guess at Hetty's feelings, and wonder how much these lines could account for Hetty leaving Paris, and even Philip, what had happened to him. She needed time to think and decided she would not tell her father about the letter, for now. But maybe it contained nothing he did not already know.

5.

Edy's arrival was greeted by Helena and Kenneth in much the same way as the announcement of his planned visit: her mother was girlish and delighted; her father distant, silent, disapproving. For Marie, it was a time of unparalleled pleasure. For days the pair of them could not see enough of each other, get enough of each other. For her it was his stillness, his voice, his lips, his hair, all of him, and the wonderful consolation of his presence. Now, two months later, and still she didn't want to let him out of her sight and, as far as she could tell, he felt the same way about her.

Three weeks earlier, on her birthday, Edy had said to her, You have the hair of a lion, so there must be something in it, being a Leo. They had woken to an unusually warm day. We should walk to the coast, she said, go down to the reef, it will be perfect. And it was. They had arrived carrying their sweaters and stood on the cliff top looking down at the pale green, shallow water on the reef. The holes were clearly visible, deep blue, and Marie thought she could see fish swimming around in the still water. Beyond the reef there was a small, well-shaped swell and a group of board riders paddling, turtle-like, rising and falling and waiting for the perfect configuration. There was a light offshore breeze and the tops of the waves flicked backwards, lazily. Everything was in slow motion.

This is a special day, said Edy.

They walked down the slope and along the beach, beyond the board riders.

Quickly, said Marie. Let's get wet before we get cold again. She stripped off all her clothes and waded to the edge of the nearest pool. Edy watched, delighted, as she dived in without a splash. He followed, less convinced, and shrunk with the coldness of the water on his body.

Back on the beach, they rubbed each other down, gasping for breath. It's still winter in the water, said Marie, but I love it. They dressed and wandered further along the beach, holding hands like lovers.

I know a cave, she said. Just above the high tide mark. Shall we go there?

6.

They walked down to an old house by the sea, built close to a river called Marybrook, in honour of the owner's wife. This is history in Australia, said Marie. There are plaques that tell you about the people who lived here, and when they died. And often that's all there is. Any other signs have been removed or destroyed. And look, a fig tree and a mulberry tree and a pine tree. They have left their mark, these people. And their graves are up on the hill. It's the boys who didn't survive. One child was called Hero, would you believe? He was born in April 1863 and died one year later. And there was Henry and Hugh, Alfred and Charles. But the girls, all those daughters, they lived and produced more of their kind; there must have been something wrong with the males; so sad, so many of them lived only a few weeks, or a year or two. They named a lake after that one, Hero, and a road, and a brook, so he is transformed and lives forever. They must have expected a lot of him. Can one-year-olds be heroes?

I don't want a lake named after me, said Edy.

Let's take this path, Marie said, and Edy followed. He would do whatever it was she desired.

There are stories about this place, she said, old stories, and there are older stories, before these people came.

They made their way along a narrow track through dense tea-trees until they came to a dilapidated stone cottage. Look at this plaque. The couple, the mother and the father, they were married at Wonnerup. Remember, that was where you camped by the edge of the sea and had strange dreams about a lost helmsman.

He looked at it and remained silent.

They walked alongside the rushing creek, careful to stay away from the crumbling edges. Everything was damp and water trickled over rocks or ran from crevices and down the slope of the hill above them, feeding the creek which couldn't run fast enough to get to the ocean. They came to a cave made from limestone, and inside, the roots of trees so ancient it seemed to these lovers that they belonged to a time when anything could have walked the earth, and in the still ferny dampness of it all anything could appear out of the trees lumbering towards them; or emerge from the water in the cave and, open-mouthed, consume the pair of them. Here was another plaque, a different history. It was about an Aboriginal girl who was promised to an old man, a tribal elder, whom she did not want to marry. She had wandered away and discovered this beautiful waterfall and cave, the bathing place of the moon, and it was here that she eloped with her lover, and it was here that they lived in secret. The elder was still powerful and had his revenge: the boy, Nobel, was found by a group of warriors and speared to death. The girl, Mitanne, was taken back to the camp, where she was forced to work very hard, and soon afterwards, it is said, she died of exhaustion and grief. In death she was reunited with her lover, and to this day they continue to live happily in the cave.

So you see, Edy, transgression is not always punished in ways that are successful.

No, but she should never have been promised to the old man in the first place. I don't think I like stories where dying is the answer to living, even though they have become very popular.

They made their way back along the narrow track and came again to a wide grassy clearing; they walked across it and headed towards the ocean.

7.

Marie was tired because the previous evening she had been to see Miles and tried to explain to him how things had changed since the arrival of Edy, that secret person whom she had not talked about with anyone. How can you tell a lover you are deeply fond of that there is nothing wrong with him in your eyes, nothing he could change, or should change, but that there is someone else? Someone you can't stop thinking about, can't live without unless you want to live with an emptiness that occasionally you forget about, but then comes rushing back, an impatient tide. Irresistible. The presence of emptiness forms ghost-like at the edge of your vision, with a sly, knowing look; it will not go away; it will sneak up on you when you least expect it, even when you are making love with someone else, Miles for instance (in a cottage), so kind and attentive and attractive? The evening had dragged on, the conversation going in narrowing circles, until there was an exhausted dead end, a full stop, with neither of them able to utter another word that would add anything to what had already been said. She knew she had provided no reasonable answers to Miles' questions, because there were none.

Driving home, she couldn't think straight as she rehearsed what they had said to each other. When friends or acquaintances suggested life owed them more than they already had, that somehow they *deserved* more, she would invariably lecture them on degrees of privilege. Now she thought Miles did not deserve the upset and suffering that she had, with no deliberate intent, caused him. It was not fair to him. *Life,* to the extent that it included her, was not fair to him. And she thought, too, of how she had imagined that it was Edy who was risking all in coming to see her, that she was the one who would choose to continue to be with him, or not, because she had already been hardened, tempered like iron, by her sense of betrayal when he withdrew into a world where she could not follow, and was not welcome. Now she knew differently: to say goodbye to him would be to say goodbye to her own self, her own life, and that she could not do. He was herself, and she hoped, she was himself. When they looked into each other's dark eyes, did they see only themselves reflected or did Edy/Marie loom large and separate from the mirror? None of this could she explain to Miles. As soon as she started to put it into words, she sounded hollow and foolish, as if she were making up a story that would let her off the hook because what she was claiming was special, different, extraordinary even. Her voice had changed, as if she were a child again, caught out in a dishonest act and Miles became the disapproving parent, even though that was not like him. In the end she had put her head in her hands and cried, and amid the tears felt guilty; she could see what it looked like, but it wasn't, it wasn't like that at all. Miles pulled her to him, gently, and held her and she felt better, for a moment, and then worse.

8.

Marie turned to Edy. She was pacing around the room, full of nervous energy, her head fit to bursting.

I've been reading more about the people who built that old house we visited. One of the daughters stayed on there, after the family moved to the big house, further south. She describes how lonely she felt, and how the winter storms would make her fearful that the roof would fly off. I know how she felt. And one of the boys of the family who did survive spent most of his time with the Aborigines, learning their language and customs, and they taught him how to catch fish, which he became very good at. Now, I wonder what happened to him, whether he kept that knowledge, and those connections, when he grew older?

Why is that so important?

Because it was unusual. Even now it would be a rare thing, such a connection. Just think if there were more people like him. Anyway, we do know a bit more about one of the children who didn't survive. Remember? That plaque, for the baby with the strange name, Hero? The mother suffered more from that death than from the death of other children that she'd given birth to. Apparently she was constantly thinking of this beautiful child and she was tearful, utterly miserable, obsessed, I suppose.

Sounds like postnatal depression, said Edy.

I suppose so, but also a death. I wonder why that son and not others? The Aboriginal women who knew the baby wept with her; it sounds like everyone thought he was a special child, but you would think all dead children would be special to their mothers, and maybe their fathers, although I'm not so sure about the father in this case. His solution was to take his wife on a camping trip, an arduous three days driving a horse and cart through difficult country at the beginning of winter to get to their destination. It was also a place he wanted to inspect to further his cattle run. He said he was relying on God, religion and philosophy to restore her tranquillity.

Ah, said Edy, patriarchal insight. There's nothing like it. I can tell you.

She looked at him, quizzically. Anyway, maybe it worked for a while; she recovered enough to produce more children, but she was dead at forty-two. Some of the locals called the big house they had moved to Castle Dangerous because male visitors had a habit of falling in love with one daughter or another, but the Aborigines called the cliff nearby The Dying Place.

Really? I guess the new owners didn't choose *that* for the name of their house?

No. They didn't...Do you think names matter, Edy?

Edy looked at her, into her eyes. No; I can't afford to, can I?

The names of places where we live, I mean. If we name something, do we see it differently? As if it belongs to us. Or we to it. Here, at this house, where we are living, there is no proper name, but I feel so caught up in it somehow. At nights I feel so close to winter storms, and the rush of the trees, I imagine myself simply disappearing in a whirl of leaves and twigs and salt and sea. And in summer, when the wind is in the east, from the opposite direction, off the desert which is cold at night but so hot during the day, I think of being consumed by fire.

So, you feel threatened by this place?

Yes sometimes I do, but it's not just the house. And I do attend to minor details. So, in summer, if I'm alert, I make sure my car is facing in the right direction for a quick getaway. Although nothing you do would make any difference, not really. My grandmother, the one whose house this was, she died in a bushfire and I'm fearful I'm living in her footsteps, ones that left the house for reasons we don't really understand, and walked into the path of the fire. I don't know whether she was running away from something, or running into something, like a moth, or does that amount to the same thing?

I suppose that's what we all do. Away and into. And we don't always escape. Were you close to your grandmother?

It's strange. Looking back, I think she was a rather distant figure to her grandchildren, to Nicholas and me. And yet I did feel close to her. She treated us more like adults, even when we were quite young. And then when we got older…I think she was more like a companion, really. A strong woman.

Like you?

I wish. Marie drew a deep breath; she did not know why she felt so emotional.

You know there are too many times when I think all I can do is sit and wait as if there's some burden that I can't throw off and yet I don't know what it is and then I get annoyed, angry, with myself for being so stupid, so passive. At that point I usually go for a walk in the bush, or along the coast, go into the territory that might destroy me, and then I feel better. Reality is not the problem.

Throughout the rush of Marie's words, Edy's eyes did not leave her face. He felt as if he were living these experiences with her, every change in expression, the sense of sadness and loss – or was it fear – written on her body. Her cottage was not a castle, but there were moments when it, too, felt dangerous.

Do you remember telling me your childhood nicknames? he asked. Dangerous and Dare? She looked at him, puzzled for a moment. Then he wrapped his arms around her and drew her to him. He could feel the softness of her and did not want to let go.

9.

Marie realised that the tiredness of the last few weeks had not left her and her breasts were tight against her bra. When Edy placed his hands on them, they were sensitive, even sore. When she walked, they tingled. There were other signs.

Do you know what this means, Edy? Something not planned – or unplanned. Did we forget what we were doing?

For a moment Edy looked surprised, then he took her in his arms and whispered, I think it's wonderful, and I didn't forget, did you?

No, not really. And she held him tightly.

Edy traced his fingers over her belly, so firm and muscled. I now have a womb, she said. Uterus sounds ridiculous.

Marie was unprepared for how quickly she became in her own mind a cocoon for something precious and at the same time felt herself to be swaddled by her surrounds. World within worlds, like a babushka doll; except she did not think of the baby inside her as a miniature of herself. She had no image of it that she could summon. In the following days she felt a surge of happiness whenever she thought of herself, no longer exclusively singular, in this new body. At times she would forget, and then remember, and smile, secretly: yes, she was pregnant; she was going to be a mother, and Edy, the father. There was mystery and awe and the beginnings of discomfort.

She did not know how she would tell her parents, or really, how she would tell her father. She told herself she didn't care what he thought, she and this baby were beyond anything he could do, or say. *Yes,* that was the case; Kenneth was no longer relevant in her life, he was a spent malevolent force in a wheelchair. But for Edy it was different. In the rare meetings between the older man and the younger one there was a formality, a distance, which did not entirely mask undertones that were not pleasant. There was always tension in the room and she felt her father was just managing to keep himself under control, to stop himself from making the critical comments she felt sure he was thinking. *What is this man doing in my house, with my daughter? Will he stay forever? What work does he do? And his hair.* In these moments when she looked into Edy's eyes she could see that he had disappeared somewhere, had gone to a place that he knew of where Kenneth could not follow, and nor could she. Afterwards, when she wanted to talk, he would shrug his shoulders, give a sad-comic smile, and say there was no point.

With Helena it would be different: a baby to fuss over, to care for, to talk about with her friends. Marie could not recall her mother being pregnant, but she did remember watching, entranced, as Nicholas fed at her breast and wanting to take hold of him herself, to be the mother. Be careful, he is not one of your dolls. You can't drop him on the floor, or pull out his hair. As if she would. She looked down at her own belly, quickening, she thought. This child will know who it is, will know its true face and its place in the world. Today she would announce the news to her parents.

They had already discussed names. I think it should be called Edy, Edy Baudin, she said. At the moment there is no one to ensure the name continues, the line will die out, which I suppose should not matter, there are quite enough families in the world. But I think it would be a pity if *you* didn't live on, Edy, so some other person, in another generation, gets to experience how precious you are.

He told her none of what she said made sense, he wasn't even a Baudin, and anyway what if it was a girl?

That's the beauty of Edy, she said, you can't really tell. Boy or girl, Edy is fine.

I know about *your* name, he said, with mock gravity. It's a common one in France, well, everywhere I suppose. If you think of the Latin, it derives from the sea, and in the case of Mary the Virgin, the star of the sea. Is that what you are, a star over the ocean leading sailors to safety and comfort? On the other hand, if it comes from the Hebrew, Miriam, it signifies rebelliousness, bitterness. What do you think, which one is it?

What do *you* think? she said.

It's obvious, isn't it? he replied. You are both: a rebellious star.

Does that mean I lead sailors onto the rocks when I'm promising them safety? She smiled at him. I do know about my own name. There is debate about what the Hebrew means. If one accepts *perfect* or *beloved* then of course I agree with that. Even more importantly it could suggest a *wished for child*. That would give us something to think about, Edy, wouldn't it?

Come here, she said. He went to sit down by her side, but she held him and pushed her face into his belly. Can you imagine what it feels like to have a child in there?

No, of course not. There are times when I'm envious: what a tiny role men have in the production of children.

Does that make you a modern man, Edy? I wonder how my father felt about such matters. I suspect he didn't feel, or think, anything at all.

10.

Despite the chilly wind straight off the ocean, Kenneth was perspiring by the time he got to the top of the hill and eased himself onto the bench. Over the weeks and months there were more and more things he could do for himself: small triumphs over his body that, once achieved, he quickly forgot what it was like not to be able to do them. Like walk to the top of the hill for the first time since his stroke and look down and see, in one direction, his house and garden and, in the other, the roof of his mother's cottage where Marie now lived with, God forbid, that man. Kenneth was still shaken by the news of a baby. He hadn't known what to say to either of them and then Helena had started up with her oohing and aahing, already speaking baby talk, and he'd lost some of that control he'd recently gained. He'd spoken angrily.

You don't know what you're in for, he'd said. The reality of a baby is very different from any *idea* you might have about it. Just ask your mother. It's not television, you know, and children are with you forever. You are always a parent, they are always a child until someone dies – and you scarcely know each other: it's a totally crazy, irresponsible thing to do. And what do you intend to live on? Neither of you has a proper job and Edy is not even a permanent resident. He'd said a lot more in this vein then finally stopped and found all three of them staring at him as if he were some alien who had dropped in unexpectedly and they couldn't make him out, or as if he were some crazy person who should be pitied. In the end he didn't know what else he could say in order for them to take him seriously, to get the condescending look out of their eyes.

Marie, finally, had spoken and told him he was not in a position to advise *anyone* about responsible parenting, given his own appalling record of disowning his son and rejecting his daughter. That is why I can, he said. And why do I have to be in a *position* to speak commonsense?

He pulled his coat more tightly around him and wished he'd worn some gloves. Weak afternoon sunlight caught the roof of the old cottage. They'd be down there somewhere, probably in bed, no more than children in spite of their ages. It frightened him how patterns seemed to repeat from one generation to the next or, as some attested, every alternate generation, so you were likely to make the same mistakes, or the same positive moves, as your grandparents. He knew nothing of his parents' parents. Whether you needed to know your forebears, to have spent time face to face with them to come under their influence, he did not know with certainty, but suspected it wasn't the case. In fact he believed the opposite: you were most likely to repeat the behaviours you knew nothing about, especially if they were not good ones. But this.

He thought of Hetty and her life and the way it had ended and, for the hundredth time, wondered whether he was responsible for her going out into the fire, simply to avoid his visit. She could have refused to answer the door if she didn't want to see him, but he knew that was not like her; she wouldn't hide away in her own house. No matter how he looked at it, he hadn't been a good son, he had caused pain that was unnecessary, had spoiled her life when she felt happy for the first time in years with someone else, a man who now seemed to him so admirable. And yet he'd never *decided* to say things or do things that might be hurtful. It had always seemed to him that there was no other way; he was simply being himself. And now, what was he to do with

Marie, and Edy, and their godforsaken child? A nightmare. He did not feel strong enough to deal with it.

He'd been sitting still for too long, and the cold had seeped into him. He started to rise when he spied a figure walking up the track towards him. Edy.

I was just about to leave, he said. That wind.

Edy nodded. Yes, you need to be very vigorous, or else sit by a fire. Can I walk back with you? I saw you up here and wanted to talk.

Kenneth shrugged. He wasn't sure he wanted anything to do with this young man, but it was difficult to say no. I'm slow, you'll have to go at my pace, and I need to use the stick going downhill, so the path won't be wide enough for both of us. If you like we could talk when we get back to the house?

Outside is better, I think, said Edy. I have been thinking about the other night and what you said about having a baby, and I know much of it is true. It was not something that we planned, but nor did we plan not to have a child. I think you know I love Marie –

– Yes, yes, I'm sure you do. And she loves you. And all my life it's what I believe *should* be between two people who wish to spend their lives together. Far too many couples do little more than tolerate each other, which is often not very attractive, and they've been like that from the beginning. Blind to what is really motivating them. No, it's not that I doubt that you love each other. There's more at stake, more than you can imagine; couldn't you have waited awhile before going ahead with a child? As I said before, a child is forever, until someone dies.

Of course we do not plan to die. I don't think I understand why you feel so strongly. Did you plan your own children?

In the beginning, yes. But then, no. It's complicated. That is one reason why I think you need to be careful, not rush, not do things that will cause pain to yourselves and others...I must get back, it's freezing up here.

Edy was silent as Kenneth began his awkward journey down the hill. He did not want to speak to the man's back, but said, It is strange, don't you think, the French connection? Your father and mother: me and Marie?

Kenneth called out over his shoulder, I have no problems with the French. How could I? I often think it's a pity they didn't stay around here a bit longer when they first arrived. All we have is a few names, largely forgotten. What if they'd hoisted the flag?

When they got to the bottom of the hill, he turned to Edy with that fierce look in his eye and said, Please don't go ahead with the child. Talk to Marie.

As Kenneth made his way slowly towards the house, he began to feel light-headed and unsteady on his feet. He thought of Chrys and her letter and could no longer block out the knowledge that had begun as a feeling that he could not give a name to, but now he knew and did not know what to do. His hands shook and then his whole body began to tremble. At the door he called out to Helena.

II.

What Edy most loved about Marie was their silences. With other friends, and girlfriends, he always felt a need, after a certain amount of time had passed, to say something. He would then have to think of what to say, and the words that came out were ones that he had no attachment to: sometimes he said silly things, things he didn't mean, occasionally hurtful, or the reverse of what he really thought. He suspected there was a critical length for a pause that probably differed from culture to culture, rather like personal physical space. How close could you stand to another person before there was discomfort? How long was a pause before tension arose? He didn't know, and with Marie the question did not arise. From the beginning both of them knew that pauses did not have to be filled and he was greatly comforted by this because although he enjoyed talking, not only to Marie, but many different people, most of all he liked to speculate and to make himself and the world around him through language. Words provided form and meaning and the capacity to reflect. This was not the sort of talk to fill spaces, or not social spaces, where there was awkwardness and obligation. The talk which brought Edy into existence required empathy and engagement but not necessarily careful listening to the meaning of the words; you needed to catch the tone and rhythm, to be swept along, to be brought to a sudden halt, to laugh, to feel frightened and joyful, to want to reach out and touch the other person with a smile, or tears, to feel that you were in it together, without knowing for certain what the 'it' was.

When he spoke some of this aloud to Marie, she said, When you rejected me you said something very different. You accused me of breaking the moment between us through words and questions. I remember. At first Edy looked surprised and then he told her he had said the opposite to what he believed because they were the only words he could grasp, the only words he could find to try to end the relationship. But also that was a different sort of talk, pragmatic. He said, I thought we both felt too strongly; I had lost all control and I was frightened. I felt I needed to sever the connection. But I didn't expect you to believe what I was saying. Or accept it. So I could say to myself that I had tried, and failed.

Oh, and now? she asked.

Now I feel strong. I have the courage to be with you and not fear being burned up in the process. And you?

I have never been frightened, not in that way. I did not want to leave.

12.

Then Edy began to wonder. Kenneth's talk about the baby had worried him. There were practical problems that he had raised: money, visas, work, where to live, how to live – surely, nothing insurmountable. And yet he'd begun to have his doubts about the wisdom of a child. He dwelt on his own childhood and the polite, distant man he called *papa* who, it seemed to him, had never changed in the whole time he had known him, from when he was a baby to a man. Is that what being a parent was about? Is that what being a child and a man was about? What did he know about such matters, when neither of his parents were his parents? He thought Ghislaine the perfect mother, and yet she had not given birth to him. *Mama, papa,* the sounds a baby might make, and that is what he felt like. He was not grown-up enough to have a child which, at his age, made him think he would never be truly adult. How could you be a child and a parent at the same time? How could you be nearly thirty and a child? He could not make sense of it.

That night, in bed, he felt frightened in ways that he hadn't experienced since childhood; his chest felt tight and his head and neck. He did not want to look into the corners of the room. He could sense some dark, intense presence lurking just below the window. It belonged somewhere in the distant past. He must stare straight ahead. He was, ridiculously, scared of the dark and too on edge to say anything to Marie in case she confirmed his fears. But tomorrow he must talk to her and avoid abstractions.

———

Marie looked at the strange man in front of her.

You have listened to my father, who knows nothing about children, you have thought about your own childhood which, by your own admission, was a happy one, and you have reached the conclusion that you don't want this baby? What has happened to you, Edy? None of this makes sense. I think you have no idea what you are asking me to do. It is not possible. If you feel you cannot be a father to this child, then you must leave. In the end, it is my body, my child, my decision. For me, there is *nothing* to think about. Edy, you are repeating what happened before; we reach a certain point and then you reject me.

Edy stood there, pale, ghostly, as if the life had been sucked out of him. I think it's wrong to have this child. Look at us. Look what we've come to.

Edy, you are taking notice of a man who is quite unbalanced. He is still obsessed by his mother, a strange mixture of guilt and blame, at his age. He has a pathological fear of change, or anything that challenges his authority. Why would you listen to him?

I know what you are saying is true, but I have this awful sense that he knows something that is appalling, something that has little to do with what you are talking about. And it affects us. I cannot really think about it, not sensibly. I have a feeling of panic inside me.

———

After a winter of low rainfall, spring arrived early and so did the bushfires. Castle Dangerous burnt to the ground, but no one was killed or injured.

FIVE

Look at the two of you, her friends had said. In London.

You can't marry, her father said. Can't you see that?

Marie sat in the dirt and looked at the weathered headstone. Nearly one hundred and fifty years later and here he was, *Hero*, still living at least in her mind and who knew how many others'? It was not clear whether the handyman turned gravedigger turned stonemason had wobbled with his tools, or the soft stone had eroded over time so the 'o' was now 'a', Hero became Hera, but what difference did it make? Had they leaked in here, too? It was Kenneth who spat out, It's the Greeks, check the Greeks, they've always known about such matters, the most beautiful and the most frightening. She had, and he was right. She discovered that Zeus had married his sister Hera. And all the contradictions of the world were focussed here. He was a trickster, constantly unfaithful, madly in love, violent. She likewise. And yet theirs was accorded a sacred marriage. She was the goddess of women and marriage; she was worshipped as a virgin. One of her daughters was the goddess of discord, another the goddess of childbirth. On it went. It seemed the Greeks had no problem with conflict and contention, with oppositions that were intolerable. Their gods were human and omnipotent, omniscient and ignorant, loving and vengeful, male and female. They consumed their children and consummated marriage with them. What people were they who created such stories to live by? Today, she thought, we demand simple stories of good and bad, right and wrong, that are pure fantasy, impossible guides in a parallel universe. We survive through disconnection. Then again, maybe Zeus and Kenneth, she could see the connection there, see his appeal. And what about Hetty? She would have been a good ancient Greek. And the child? It would have had a Greek grandmother, so it seemed.

What Marie knew now was that Hero's mother and father had a body to bury and a place to come to. She knew it took a long time to be born, to live and die, nine months, even a child not properly formed. There were nightmares, it was still growing inside her. Soon she would feel it beginning to move, right on time. Betrayed again by her body. A trick of the mind. She would wait, anxiously. She would give birth; it would draw breath, move its tiny limbs, cry, and then die. She needed to see it through.

The wind had died down and all she could hear was the sound of the ocean and the occasional call of a bird that she could not see. For a while she was absorbed into the silence and weight of the moment and then her mind started to intrude, a voice that was at first a murmur and then gathered strength: you are a fraud, a pretender, contriving grief, thieving another's life, and death. She got to her feet and dusted herself down, picking the ants off her that had begun to crawl up her legs. She was at a complete loss; there was nothing that she could think of, nothing that she wanted to do; so she would walk back down the hill to the sea.

Everything was still, as if waiting for something to happen. She stayed away from the road and made her way through the sparse bush, blackened in part from the recent fires. At the bottom of the hill she walked across what had been, originally, a paddock for the cows and entered a narrow track, well worn, by the side of the river. Here the vegetation was dense and some of it was beginning to flower. She was assailed by the sweet musky smell of the coast. She met no one on her way and when she arrived at the point where the river, really no more than a creek, pushed its way into the ocean, she followed its rocky path through the beach sand and stood barefoot in the chilly shallows where the fresh water, stained brown, mixed with the surge of the ocean. She marvelled at the fierceness of the flow of the creek, the Marybrook, as it entered the sea, which seemed intent on keeping it out as wave after wave crashed onto the beach. It was a battle the ocean couldn't win, not at this time of the year. When summer returned and the creek slowed, becoming no more than a series of still, brown pools, the sand bar would build up again and the two bodies of water would become separate. Life on the land side would go into hiding, remaining still and quiet, while the ocean would maintain its restlessness, always impatient to be doing something different. It's like an adolescent, she thought, always asking *what now? what now? what's new?* Whereas in summer the land was like an old man or woman wise and resilient, knowing that not everything happened in the moment. Memory counted for something; you lived in layers of time and experience, layers which seeped into each other.

Star of the sea, Edy had called her. If she'd had something to bury, would she have chosen the land or the sea, the earth or the ocean? Both would be there for a long time, longer than any of them. The land had echoes, but if you had nothing but memories, you couldn't bury them; perhaps they could be scattered into the air and the waves, you could enter that energy, now, and in years to come the voice would diminish, the cry become so faint you could scarcely hear it. Dust to dust, ashes to ashes. She needed to do something; there had to be a way of living where you were not doubled over in pain beyond imagining, where your mind and body had collapsed and you lay there in the dark not wanting to see the sky begin to lighten, where you cursed the pre-dawn mutterings of birds, and pulled the blanket over your head, thinking if you could just hold your breath, hold your breath, then there would be an end.

Fully clothed, she walked into the water until the waves forced her to push up firmly from the sea floor; she did not want to be swamped by the ocean. She gasped and stepped further out. On tiptoes, she could not open her mouth. Then, arms outstretched, Marie floated. The tension seeped out of her. I am not a madwoman, she murmured to the overarching blue. Then the coldness of the water reached her bones.

She turned her back on the ocean and the creek; she began to walk inland. Her wet clothes chafed. She decided to ignore the track and began taking whatever paths of least resistance were presented to her, animal paths of one kind or another, that headed more or less in the right direction. Half an hour later and she was not back at the grassy paddock near the old house at the bottom of the hill. She knew she was not seriously lost because she hadn't gone in circles and headed back to the ocean, but nor had she gone in a straight line, eastwards, which is what she had intended. She came to a slight rise where there were no trees, only the low, aromatic bushes, so she was walking parallel to the coast, still on sparsely vegetated sand-dune country. All she could see in the direction she wanted to go in was the scrubby outline of the snug hills and she could hear the sound of the waves breaking on the shore behind her. In the stillness, there was nothing: she was not there in that moment. It could have been a thousand years ago. Then, much further away than she thought, she spied it, the foreigner, the height and colour and shape, all so different. The Norfolk Island pine, planted near the house. A stranger after one hundred and fifty years and that was the direction she needed to go in. The settlers had left their mark.

Further down the coast, out of sight, the Dying Place was grey sand, blackened trees, stick figures, ash.

2.

For Edy, these were the worst of times. He was not sure the fragments of himself would ever reassemble into something resembling a whole. How could he explain to Marie that he didn't know, but he knew? Knowledge like water that seeped into parched earth, or the trunk of a dead tree, month after month, it got closer to the centre. And then. He came to believe that he possessed, initially, a cellular knowledge that only gradually became part of his conscious mind, so he was constantly doing things that he did not know the meaning of, did not know the why behind the what. Why had he come all this way to Australia to see Marie, beyond the fact that she was part of him, a familiar limb of his body that he could not do without? That seemed like a perfectly good reason and yet all the while there was something beyond the perfectly good, a shadow territory that he was aware of, but could never bring into focus. He saw himself as a swimmer who duck dives beneath the surface of the ocean, where for the first metre or so the water is clear and the deeper you go, the murkier it becomes. You know with certainty there is an ocean floor, not far away, but you can't see it until you are so close that you can touch it. You have to push through the murk, not knowing what it contains or hides, and for Edy that uncertainty was frightening. He imagined creatures that were harmful, that could bite, or sting, or poison. There would be weed that you could become entangled with, rocks with shells so sharp they would slice through your skin and make you bleed. He convinced himself that there were good reasons for not going down too deep, not getting out of your depth, and then felt guilty about his cowardice. Now he was being punished for an ignorance that was not entirely wilful, but he felt he had turned away, glanced in the opposite direction, without knowing that he had chosen to do so at the very time he should have looked firmly forward, seen what was in front of his eyes. And hers. When he had told her he did not want to see her again. And then his mind changed. The punishment did not stop with himself. Grief now had a body and a face contorted almost beyond recognition. He wondered whether Marie would ever get over what they had done. They were not the first human beings to say they did not know, they did not intend, and went ahead with the unthinkable. We did not choose. But there was a choice. Was it their future, or the child's future that they envisaged? What would people think? screamed Helena. She was shaking with fury and fear. Kenneth was silent, and grey. There was no one else he could blame.

Edy had begun to gather up his few belongings, to place them in the hallway, packed, ready to go. This much he had to do. It was a signal to himself that he could not stay; he did not know where he would go, presumably London, or even Paris. Not because he wanted to be in either place, but he couldn't think of an alternative.

3.

Nothing he'd said had made any difference. Now he was certain. Now they had to know. The voice from his twisted body shook. Look at the pair of you, can't you see why you cannot have this child? Edy could feel the panic in Marie as they stood there, arms loosely on each other's hips. As for this latest idea, that you are going to get married, it's against the law, Kenneth whispered. He'd turned his back on them and made his way out of the room, his gait awkward. He stumbled and reached for the doorframe. He turned and stared at the three of them. A brother cannot marry his sister, nor a sister her brother. Surely you knew?

That night on their way home they walked away from the path, lay beneath the trees on a carpet of sheoak needles, and held each other; the days that followed were, truly, a nightmare. They were awake at all hours, unhinged by their dreams, monstrous like the ones you have as a child when sick with fever. They would wake, shocked and frightened, always cowering from the pursuit by shapes, rolling wheels and circles that grew bigger by the moment and threatened to overtake them, haul them into a world that was animate, cold, and unsafe. In spite of the chill, when they awoke from their dark world they would be sweating and desperate and discover that their fears were identical, they had dreamt the same nightmare. The daylight hours were not much better. They had dark circles under their eyes and looked haggard and distracted. Edy and Marie abandoned words entirely and began sleeping in separate beds. They knocked on the door of the big house and told their father, mother, and stepmother, that they had decided to go ahead and have the child. There would be no abortion. Helena went crazy and they stood there and watched her, unable to feel shock or surprise. They held each other as they walked back to the cottage. They lit the fire and sat there, silent and cold. Edy went out to the woodpile and gathered the largest and driest pieces and piled them into the fireplace. In time it began to blaze and slowly the room warmed up and for the first time in days they began to think of food and Marie decided she would risk a glass of wine.

In the big house, cold and empty, Kenneth told Helena about what was in the note he'd received all those years ago from Chrysanthe. She'd taken the child to France, to be adopted by some friends of hers. The fact that he was adopted was not to be a secret, but there were to be no details provided about his biological parents. It was one of many mistakes, he said. When I first saw him, I think I went into some sort of shock. Then rejected what my eyes were telling me. I waited for someone else to comment. But it did not happen, not like that. And then one day I saw him at a little distance and noticed the movement of his hands, his walk, the turn of his head and I could no longer pretend. He reminded me so much of my mother. Surely I was not the only one to see the person in front of us?

A week later, Marie began to bleed, her face as white as the notepaper on her desk. She did not stop. The doctors told her there was nothing they could have done.

4.

Kenneth had waited until the sun was a bit stronger and the cool wind from the east had lost its edge before setting out. Now he walked along the bitumen road that ran past his mother's cottage. If they happened to be at the window, looking out, they would see him. He stared straight ahead. His pace was slow, but he felt safe enough; cars were few and he didn't think it was likely he would stumble and fall, although walking too close to the edge of the road where the gravel joined the black top made him uneasy. He had woken up with the determination that today he would walk in his mother's footsteps, he would follow the path that he'd avoided, the one she must have taken on the day she walked out of the house shortly before he was due to arrive.

He wondered what his mother would have thought about this diabolical situation. He discovered that he was shaking his head in disbelief at the thought that she would not have been shocked. He walked slowly past the house, surreptitiously glancing sideways at the vacant windows; or that's what he thought he saw, nobody there. Certainly no movement. He could feel a tightness in his chest and its gradual movement up through his neck and shoulders and then it lodged behind his eyes and stayed there. For days he had felt his mother was to blame for what had happened with Edy and Marie, and that he needed to take this walk to work out why he was convinced that what was wrong now was all due to what had been wrong in the past. He didn't know what all the connections were between the bits of this diagram in his mind – figures in circles – but he knew there *were* connections and what he needed was a clear head to work them out. Hetty, his father Fredric, his aunt Henrietta, himself, Andrew. And then Philip. Marie and Edy. And what about Nicholas? The empty circle was his father, and that was his mother's fault. It was Hetty's decision, decades ago, to leave him and Paris – and now Paris had come back to haunt them. Fate, aided and abetted by that selfish and indulgent woman, his mother, was nasty and vengeful. There was nothing you could do to fight it. There was nothing he could have done. He would never understand. Somewhere back in time an imbalance had been created and this was the shockwave, still travelling, on and on.

Before setting out, he'd tried to talk to Helena about his sense of entrapment, the feeling that he was powerless within this web of people and circumstance. She'd said, But Paris has not come back. Not really. And Chrysanthe, the choices you made then? How do you account for that? Or do you refuse to accept –

That is not where it began, he'd loudly replied, you must go further back.

He reached the footpath that bisected the cape and was a shortcut to the town. Back then it was a dirt track that anyone on foot would have used, unless they had a good reason not to. Probably more people walked in those days, so it would have been well worn, but if Hetty hadn't taken the shortcut, she would have been alright; she'd gone the wrong way.

The sun was now high in the blue sky and he was beginning to feel hot in his jacket but he would find it awkward to take it off and then he would have to carry both it and his walking stick, so he left it on. The bush here was not so thick and he imagined he could still see signs of the fire that had killed Hetty. Some burnt blackbutt trunks and blackboys without dense skirts of dead spiky leaves. He refused to call these familiar, ancient forms xanthorrhoea; it sounded too foreign to him. There were marri and jarrah trees with scorched bark, faded but still visible. Dotted throughout were occasional patches of yellow and purple, early blooming wattles and hardenbergia creepers hanging down from trees and covering bushes. Spring was a glib season, he thought.

He knew where the body had been found, about midway along the path. He had been told that there had been some damage to the flesh, especially her face. Her hair had disappeared and her eyes had been burnt. It could not have been nice, yet her body wasn't charred *beyond recognition,* as they say. She'd probably died of smoke inhalation, or maybe her heart gave out; she was an old woman. Like he was an old man. He thought of that vague empty space, neither light nor dark, *death*, something this day was happily ignoring in its apparent cheerfulness. As he approached the bend where he knew his mother had been found, his heart started to beat more fiercely and his body became tense. This made no sense to Kenneth. He kept on and noticed there was something in the very spot where the body had been lying. Someone had put a park bench there. Well, that was okay, a good place to sit and have a rest. Then he noticed the small plaque: *In Memory of Hetty D'Anger, 1919–2010.* He paused, staring at the bench as if it were a strange object and he unable to decipher its meaning. His brother's doing; no one else could be responsible for this and, as usual, he had not been informed. Hetty and Andrew conspiring again, excluding him from their arrangements, their little understandings. He was about to move on, but changed his mind and sat on the bench, his back against the plaque. Then he began to shake, his whole body uncontrollable, tears from nowhere; he bent over, two hands holding onto his stick to stop himself from falling off the bench. If he could have, he would have curled up there, like a child. What on earth was happening to him, he could scarcely breathe, what was wrong with him? He began to feel frightened.

He sat there for a long time before trying to get to his feet and beginning the journey home. He remembered another journey with the sharp recall of age, his mother's hair touching his face, the sound of her voice in the warm room with the fire going. He could feel the cream being rubbed on the bloody graze as he looked up at her, twisting his arm to see how badly hurt he was. She kissed the top of his head and he felt pleased and did not move. And then everything changed, forever, it seemed. Eventually he calmed down and as he took his first tentative steps he thought of his son, Nicholas, and did not know why. Some time soon he would go and see him.

5.

Helena knew that Edy was by himself. She walked up the hill and by the time she arrived felt light-headed and a little breathless. She knocked and let herself into the house. It was still and quiet and then she heard Edy's footsteps in the kitchen. He entered the passageway and they stood there, saying nothing. Helena looked at him, shook her head, tried to say what she had planned and then started to cry. Edy did not know what to do. There were tears in his eyes as he watched her. He wanted to comfort her, for the pair of them to hold on to each other, but he did not dare. Helena ran her hand down her face and turned away. It is not your fault, she said, but you cannot stay here. You must leave, as soon as possible. She walked to the door, half turned towards him and said, I am sorry. He watched the door close behind her.

6.

It was still dark and there were people in the room who were unhappy; her eyes remained closed as she tried to grasp who they were, to take them out of the shadows. Then the disturbing sound of the kookaburras which didn't belong here, calling one to another, an unearthly laugh at this hour, and probably the cause of her waking. She reached out for Edy, slid her hand beneath the sheets to feel his warmth – and felt the coldness of the empty space. Her body lurched and she tightened herself into a ball. The moonlight gleamed on the floorboards; down the passageway and off to the right she thought she could hear his troubled breathing. Marie could feel the stillness of the approaching day and listened to the muffled roar of the ocean in the distance. There was always the sea. She wasn't likely to go back to sleep, but it was too early to get up, and too cold: she would have to lie there in that in-between state of wanting and not wanting to get out of bed. She knew these moments could become intolerable, and she would have to fill her mind with some image, or event, or place that felt good or otherwise be overcome with anxiety. She thought of Edy lying between her legs delicately kissing her belly, her empty belly, his hair tickling her skin. She wanted to go to him, to hold him, to feel safe again. Her legs began to tingle uncomfortably; she threw off the bedclothes and grabbed a T-shirt, blouse and track top still inside each other and pulled them on in one quick movement. Then the bottoms. Then her thick socks and Rossi boots.

Outside there was the glow of false dawn in the eastern sky. Her feet crunched on the gravel as she walked to her car. Inside, the seats and even the steering wheel were cold; she turned the heater onto full and was blasted by chill air. She drove through the trees, shadows leaping in the headlights. When she reached the bitumen she continued to drive slowly; there were no other cars on the road but it was a bad time of the day for kangaroos which were difficult to see in the half-light on the verges and could jump out at you without warning. She could not imagine how she would deal with one injured and bleeding, gasping for breath by the side of the road. She would have to drive on and leave it and days later spy it obscenely bloated, legs extended, with flies and crows in attendance.

———

She found a branch of a peppermint tree about the thickness of her finger and after a small struggle broke it off. She took it to the woodheap and chopped off a length a little longer than her middle finger. When she peeled the bark off with a knife she was surprised at the wetness of the wood beneath, smooth and pink like a limb. She worked with a small curved chisel, very sharp, paring away at the wood which was much harder than she expected. A simple torso was established by carving off the rounded section of the lower half of her tree limb. She then dug out tiny indentations all the way down so her figure was clothed and buttoned. The head and eyes were rudimentary. Below the neck she used a knife to remove a squared section that would allow her to glue another piece into place for the arms, a dry twiggy piece of the tree. She worked slowly, making a doll that was primitive in every sense. That did not concern Marie, or the fact that she was once again trying to find solace in the practice of others. At the very least she would have an object that she could carry in her pocket, run her fingers around its shape, feel the cool smoothness of the back, pinch it so hard that she might be able to stop the tears that surprised her and, on occasion, embarrassed her. She had begun to feel that she had no right to continued grief, feared that she was beginning to take a peculiar pleasure in the extremity of her situation. At moments she could stand aside and tell the bizarre story of Edy and Marie, two characters fated to live out old stories embedded, shockingly, in the culture. She was a figure of mythic proportions, Hera to Edy's Zeus, blinded by Aphrodite, lying in a bed of clover and crocuses. What could either of them have done? And now, more importantly, what were they to do next?

CODA

Look at us, they said.

Marie sat on the edge of Edy's bed and threaded his hair off his face; she kissed him on his forehead.

What? he said.

I don't think it makes any difference. How are we changed? Why can't we be the same people before we found out about...She hesitated.

About the fact that we have the same father, we are brother and sister, that our relationship is incestuous? His tone was sharp, but then his voice dropped as if suddenly exhausted. How *can* this make no difference? We are not the same people we were last month. We *can't* be, even if it takes time for us to catch up to those new selves.

He looked into her eyes for a moment and then pulled the sheet over his head. Marie put her hand on the outline of his shoulder: he felt like a piece of iron.

I think we will eventually get used to the idea, get over the shock. We can't go from loving each other one day to saying we will have nothing more to do with each other the next, as if we can *decide* to turn ourselves into strangers. She paused before continuing. I didn't keep thinking of you the whole time you were in London, and I was here, and you didn't come all this way to Australia for no reason. It's because we believed we couldn't live without each other. Separated, we don't know who we are, we don't know *how* to live. Don't you see that, Edy? Don't you see that beneath the surface of this horrible, unimaginable mess we *are* the same as we were before?

I think it will only get worse, Edy muttered beneath the sheet.

Marie pulled it back from his face. I need to look at you when you are talking. Why will it get worse?

That's what will happen. The reality of brother and sister will sink in and take us down. Slowly, we will begin to look at each other and say, I have found my lost brother/sister and I'm sure we will like each other very much, feel grateful for the discovery. But you don't have a child with your sister, you don't go to bed with your sister, you don't live with your sister in that way.

As he spoke, Marie looked away. You're wrong, she whispered. I know you're wrong. That's not how it will be, at all. You can't have what we have had, what we still have, and pretend otherwise.

All colour had drained from her face. Edy shifted over and pulled back the bedclothes. She hesitated, then joined him. They lay together in the warmth, Edy holding her from behind. After a while he whispered in her ear, I have to go.

No, she said. Stay a bit longer.

I mean I have to leave here, leave this country, leave you, he replied.

After a moment she said: But we are your family, you have found not only a sister, but a father.

No, said Edy. He is not my father and never will be, and as yet you're not my sister. I want to leave before that happens. I want to remember us as we are. Perfect.

That might damage you forever, said Marie. Ruined by the thought of perfection, an ideal that could never exist, and didn't exist because what we had was not real.

I thought you said –

Not looking at him, she put her hand over his mouth. Shh. What if we left here, lived somewhere else, started off again, away from our father who art in heaven? If there is no one to tell us we are brother and sister, then we need not be. We can be whatever we like, the perfect couple. What's dangerous is to hold onto that idea when we are apart, thousands of miles away, we would live virtual lives until we got old and grey and died, still thinking of each other. You would go mad, you'd be like Heathcliff in that novel, and I'd be Cathy's ghost, haunting your dreams. We would not live peacefully.

For a while they lay there in silence, listening to the wind. I would be doing what Hetty, my grandmother, did, said Marie. After Philip died, a man she really loved, the rest of her life was framed by memory, a past she regarded as perfect and irreplaceable. So she stayed there and I think it's why women became her close friends, no longer men. She had energy, Hetty, but always stood just outside of herself; she couldn't hide the sadness that surrounded her. I suppose in the end she did give up. Maybe she believed she was joining Philip, or another dear friend, Henrietta, although I doubt it; I don't know, but I do know it's not the way I'm going to live.

In the passageway, the phone started to ring. They looked at each other. In the silence it sounded very loud; it rang again and again and then stopped.

Edy's arms tightened around her. There is no answer, there is no way out, he said, once again in a whisper, as if he could scarcely speak. Then he continued, I think of Timothée Vasse, dried up and sunburnt on a beach, spat out by this country, deserted, unable to leave, unable to stay, watching the horizon day after day, hoping to be rescued.

Yes, said Marie. And yet all the while safety was in his own hands. He needed to look to where he was, not to where he was not. Water, food, fish, companionship, it was all there. You told me that. He forgot where he was, and that's why he died.

She turned her body to him. We too can be gods and we won't forget where we are, will we Edy?

He paused for a long time, looking into her eyes and seeing there the dark reflections. He took in a deep breath. No, he said, we won't. And kissed her.

Once again the phone started up. Marie roused herself and walked down the passageway, the ringing insistent and loud, filling the space around her. At first there was silence, then Helena spoke, her voice low. It's your father, she said. You must come.

ACKNOWLEDGEMENTS

Thank you to the readers of various drafts of this work: Susan Midalia, Robyn Mundy and Amanda Curtin – for comments thoughtful, perceptive and always helpful. I'm grateful for the presence of writerly friends and companions: Annabel Smith, Vahri McKenzie, Danielle Wood, Nicole Sinclair and Donna Mazza. And very special thanks to Britta Kuhlenbeck.

A mere 'thank you' is not sufficient to measure the gratitude felt to Terri-ann White and UWA Publishing for their ongoing support. But here it is: Thank you Terri-ann.

I would also like to thank Katie Connolly, a thoughtful and sensitive editor.

The epigraph is from Anne Michael's *The Winter Vault,* Bloomsbury Publishing, London, 2009.